MW01503905

A PIRATE'S TREASURE

SCOTTISH ROGUES OF THE HIGH SEAS

BOUNTIES, BEAUTIES, &ROGUES

What happens when a mercenary gets more than he bargains for?

Pirate mercenary Lochlan MacLean loves his life on the sea, yet yearns for lands of his own to call home. He chooses his missions wisely, taking care they don't go against his strict moral code. But when a deceitful father hires him for a challenging task - kidnapping a woman - he questions himself and his ethics. The spoils in both land and coin will fulfill his dream, and he can't resist the job or the beautiful lass.

Strong-willed Lady Isobel Willys has always been promised her future is hers to choose until her father betrays her by promising her to a widowed Scottish laird under the guise of a peace treaty between their borderland families. While journeying to visit family, her travel party is set upon by a handsome highlander who she believes is her betrothed too impatient to wait. Soon she finds out everything she's ever known is a lie and her family's future is uncertain.

Isobel's fierce attraction to Lochlan threatens the promised peace for her family. She must make a choice: go against her family's wishes to live the life she chooses, or lose the man she might be in love with. Lochlan's desire for Isobel could cost him lands and coin. Can he give up the one thing he's always wanted for the one thing he never knew he needed?

A PIRATE'S TREASURE

BRENNA ASH

Enjoy the
adventure!

PRAISE FOR BRENNA ASH

"Ms. Ash does a masterful job of transporting the reader onto the ship and into this period of piracy and treachery."
— InD'tale Magazine (A Pirate's Wrath)

"Wonderful action and danger in this well-written tale you will get lost in this author's style of writing."
— Goodreads reviewer (A Pirate's Wrath)

"CAPTURED BY THE MERCENARY will sweep you aboard a pirate ship on the high seas - Prepare for lots of fast-paced action, adventure, and a lovely romance to unfold!"
— Amazon reviewer (Captured by the Mercenary)

"A fun high seas adventure that historical readers will absolutely love."
— Goodreads reviewer (A Pirate's Treasure)

A Pirate's Treasure
Brenna Ash

Copyright © 2021 by Brenna Ash
Dark Moor Media, LLC

This book is a work of fiction. Names, characters, places, and incidents are the product of the author's imagination or are used fictitiously. Any resemblance to actual events, locales, or persons, living or dead, is coincidental.

ALL RIGHTS RESERVED. No part or the whole of this book may be reproduced, distributed, transmitted, or utilized (other than for reading by the intended reader) in any form or by any means without prior written permission by the author. The unauthorized reproduction or distribution of this copyrighted work is illegal, and punishable by law.

Cover Design: Dar Albert, Wicked Smart Designs

Editor: Erica Monroe, Quillfire Author Services

ISBN: 978-1-955677-01-1

～

To Chelle, for introducing me into this wickedly fun world of pirates. Without your persuasion, this series wouldn't exist.

～

CHAPTER 1

Lanercost, England
1484

*I*sobel Willys watched her father, Lord James Willys, pace the floor of the parlor, his beefy hands fisted behind his back, a serious look darkening the features of his weathered face.

She sat on a cushioned chair, waiting for her father's news. He'd arrived home not long ago after traveling for a sennight and stated he had important information to share. She hadn't the faintest idea of what he was talking about, but his countenance as he continued to pace had her worried.

He glanced at her mother, Lady Anne, before stopping in front of Isobel. His look made her uncomfortable for reasons she couldn't understand. Had something happened?

James rocked his feet from heel to toe a few times before finally speaking. "I've secured a husband for you. A marriage that will benefit both our families." He said firmly.

Isobel blinked. Once. Twice. Unsure if she'd heard him correctly.

"James," her mother warned. "We've talked about this. You were not to make any decisions without consulting me first." There was something in the way her mother spoke. Anne had an air of authority about her. A regality her father had never possessed. "You've offered no prospects before now."

Her father had the good grace to look ashamed, while Isabel's stomach dropped.

Married? She didn't need a husband. Nor did she want one. Hadn't her mother always told her she could pick her husband? That such a burden would never be forced upon her? Was this a sick joke her father was playing? Just another way for him to torment her?

She'd not put it past him.

James cleared his throat. "The marriage will proceed as planned. It has already been agreed upon, and the contracts are signed." He approached Isobel and grasped her arm roughly. "You will marry," he ordered. "And you will not bring shame upon your family by refusing."

She jerked her arm away. "I will not." She looked to her mother, her eyes pleading with the woman to put a stop to whatever plan had been put in motion without her knowledge or consent. "Mother," she choked out, but her mother didn't respond. Anne stood there, hands fisted at her sides, staring at James as if he weren't even there. As if she were looking right through him.

Would she allow this?

Her father stepped forward again, backing her up against the wall, his cruel brown eyes darkening to black as his fingers dug painfully into her shoulders.

"James," her mother bellowed and stepped forward grabbing his arms. "Do not lay your hands on her."

He let Isobel go and stepped back, shooting a fierce look to Anne before addressing Isobel again. "You will do as you're told. For once in your life, you will obey. Since your uncle's death and your upcoming travels to pay your respect, your future husband has agreed to delay the ceremony until after you and your mother have returned. Then which you will be married."

"James," her mother repeated. "What have you done?"

"What needed to be done. Isobel cannot live out her days here with us. She needs to forge an alliance. To do her part. And soon, she'll be too old to wed. This is a good match. The best she can expect to see, really, given her age." His beady eyes roamed over her disdainfully as if the sight of her made him physically ill.

Isobel wasn't one to cry, but she couldn't stop the tears that threatened to spill. She'd been raised to believe that her life was her own. That no one would make that type of decision for her. Marriage hadn't been the subject of any of their recent conversations. Why was it suddenly a necessity to be pushed through so quickly?

She swiped at the tears dampening her cheeks and sniffed. She couldn't believe this was happening.

"Stop crying!" He began to once again pace the floor of the parlor, fists clenched at his sides. "This *will* happen."

Isobel flinched, squeezing her eyes shut and wishing she was any place else but here.

Anne stepped forward, and her blue eyes narrowed on her husband. "Pray tell, who is this man that you've deemed worthy enough of our daughter that you would go against our agreement?"

Isobel watched the exchange between her parents. Their behavior alluded to an unspoken issue. There was more to

3

this discussion, but she had no idea as to what that could be. Her mother had always been open with her. James always kept her at a distance. He'd always had a mean streak, bordering on cruel, but had never physically hurt her.

"What agreement?" Isobel asked, her eyes darting between her mother and James, waiting for one of them to answer.

"It's not of any importance," James stated.

"That is not for you to decide. We've always told Isobel she could choose her husband. She shouldn't be bound to a loveless marriage," she spat.

"Agreements be damned. She's had long enough and she's quite lucky I've found her a proper suitor." Walking to the sideboard, he poured himself a cup of ale and took a long sip before continuing. "He's a landowner and recently widowed. The location of his lands will combine our family's forces and make for a very strong border."

"You've promised her to a Scot?" Anne looked as if she'd been slapped as her eyes bored into her husband's, her voice laced with disgust.

"It's the best I could do. She has no dowry."

Isobel's eyes widened at that fact. "No dowry. What happened to my dowry?"

His face turned red with anger.

"You've gambled our daughter's dowry away? James?"

The man who had never really treated her as a daughter fumed at her mother's question.

"How could you? After everything else you've lost?"

Concern furrowed her brow. "Mother? What are you saying?"

"What she is saying," James ground out through gritted teeth, "is that we are low on monies. This union will restore our wealth and allow us to stay in our home. It's time you do your daughterly duty."

On and on, the battle between her parents raged. In the end, her father wouldn't budge. The union had been agreed upon and there would be no backing out.

CHAPTER 2

Sandaig Bay, Scotland

𝓛ochlan 'Chaos' MacLean sat on a piece of driftwood, surrounded by the white sands and the calming sounds of Loch Hourn as a cool breeze lifted his hair, blowing the golden strands into his eyes while he inspected the missive one of his men, Colin Harris, had handed him earlier that morning.

They'd only been docked a short while, but Honey, the pirate name Colin was known as, had managed to break away from the crew and make his way inland to retrieve the letter Lochlan knew was there waiting for him.

There was no place he'd rather be than sitting in silence by the sea, listening to the water slap against the rocks.

The sound calmed him. Freed his soul.

Since he'd been away from land for so long, sailing the open waters, it was past time for some normalcy in his life, because as much as he loved being on the *Hella*, his pirate ship, it was always nice to be on land. To walk on solid ground again.

He turned his face to the sun, absorbing its warmth and breathed in a deep cleansing breath as the salt-tinged breezed caressed his skin.

Turning his attention back to the letter, he broke the unfamiliar seal on the missive, and read the name of the sender, Lord James Willys, also unknown to him, though that wasn't uncommon. Lochlan often received letters from strangers. His life, not so much as a pirate, but as a member of the Amadán was blanketed in secrecy with plans made in the dark and behind closed doors.

Secrets and lies. That had been his life for as long as he could remember. For the most part, as long as he got paid, he didn't care. Though he did have a couple of exceptions.

Morals and ethics.

Odd traits for a pirate, but that's where the Amadán came in. They were his family. His brothers, bound not by blood, but by honor and duty.

It was the only life he'd ever known.

He glanced down at the missive once again, this time noticing something curious. The ink was smudged. Whoever drafted it was in a hurry. They hadn't allowed sufficient time for the ink to dry before handing the message off to be delivered.

Reading the words again, Lochlan studied their meaning. It was an unusual request.

"I need you to capture my daughter. Spirit her away until I make contact with you once again. She is due to be married, but refuses. This will ensure the marriage occurs as planned.

Do not harm my daughter or my wife, with whom she'll be traveling, or the deal will be void."

Lochlan ran his hands through his windblown hair. Abduct a lass? The man's own daughter no less. He understood that women sometimes didn't want to marry. And forced marriage was common, especially with wealthier families.

This mission could cause trouble for him and his crew for a lot of reasons. To name a few, women were fickle, manipulating creatures, and other than the occasional one to warm his bed he chose to keep the fairer sex at a distance. Though the thought of settling down with a wife of his own wasn't far from his mind these days.

He was a pirate and a mercenary, not a scourge for God's sake. Well, mayhap he was a scourge, but that didn't mean he targeted women, which is what this mission was asking him to do.

Of course many women had fallen into his lap over the years as spoils of war, but he always treated them with the respect they deserved. He allowed them to choose their own destinies. Never did he hurt or dishonor them.

That being said, they still didn't belong on his ship. They were a temptation his men did not need. He trusted his men, but there was only so much control they'd have depending on the length of time they'd be at sea.

But this situation...this was different.

He read on and learned his employers name and the marriage was payment for past debts. And also that the target was an English Lady. A woman of noble birth.

He would have to head into English waters, down to Solway Firth, which meant he would need to keep an eye on their surroundings.

The English wouldn't take kindly to the *Hella* sailing within their boundaries.

It would make for a dangerous journey. This wouldn't be the first time he and his men found themselves in English territory and he was certain it wouldn't be the last, but usually he wasn't hiding a woman on the *Hella* with him. That would be asking for trouble.

A noble lady, no less.

What if they were attacked? Could he protect his ship and men, knowing she was on board? And keep her safe, too? The plan would have to be well thought out.

And then there were his men.

They were a superstitious lot.

Women did not belong on pirate ships. They were bad luck. Or so the legend said.

They wouldn't take too kindly to having a female on board either. It was dangerous. Unpredictable. Not just for her, but for all of them.

Even if his crew had their fair share of wenches and ale whilst they were docked, which no doubt, they would, after several long, lonely days on the ship, they might start thinking she was there to serve a purpose.

He'd have to keep her out of sight. Mayhap locked in his quarters. The thought didn't bode well for him.

For certain, the reward he would reap would be worth sleeping below deck with his crew.

But he vowed he would return her in the same condition he'd captured her in, even if it killed him. Which it just might.

Lochlan took a deep breath and blew it out. His men knew better than to harm a woman. None wanted to face his wrath if they did.

But he had new recruits that he'd just hired. And he'd be a

fool not to assume that some of them might think with their cocks instead of their brains.

For the most part, everyone else on his ship were either mercenaries or hired pirates. Or both. He was respected as captain, but that didn't mean he didn't face a challenge from time to time, and a lass was oft the cause. It was going to be tough keeping her safe. But the coin, jewels and land were so worth the trouble.

The land especially. As the bastard son of a cook, having lands of his own was not something he would have inherited from family, even if they were close. Which they weren't. Owning land was just a dream. One that he'd been working toward ever since he could remember.

A dream that he wasn't sure he could ever fulfill.

Until now.

They would need to plan carefully and pray for a lot of luck to be successful.

He could hear his men in the distance, their voices carrying on the wind, as they made their way into town to seek the very tempting type of treasure he would have to demand they leave the hell alone once back onboard.

Lochlan thought back to his youth. Remembering the hours he'd spent at the docks, watching ships of all kinds come into port. Pirate ships included, though they mostly tended to stay further out in the open water.

He had been on his own ever since he'd been able to dress himself. Doing whatever it took to survive.

He watched in awe, dreaming that one day he would be sailing to faraway places just like they did.

And he noticed right away that these men were different from the others.

The pirates.

They were loud and boisterous, telling tales of distant places, riches beyond his imagination, and of exotic women as they sang bawdy songs that enthralled him. They were so unlike the stiff uniformed men on the royal or merchant ships, and Lochlan wanted to be just like them.

He'd spent years washing the ships, and running errands for the pirates. Not only to feed himself, but to pursue his dream of becoming one of them. He'd done whatever he could to make inroads with them. He'd watched quietly, taking everything in. He'd learned their ways. How to behave. How to talk. How to approach others. And most importantly, how to deal with someone that did you wrong.

One day, the pirate he admired the most, Allan "Thrash" MacTavish approached him, and it changed his life forever. The man had taught him so much about pirating. How to plunder.

But mostly, about honor.

It had been on one of Thrash's missions that Lochlan had gained his own ship, the *Hella*.

That day was one of Lochlan's proudest moments.

All of those things made him into the man he was today. He loved the sea. The smell of the salty air. There wasn't a scent he enjoyed more.

But even so, it didn't mean he didn't long for a place on land that he could call his own.

That's what this mission would get him. Would he be ready to lower his pirate flag and stay on dry land? He couldn't possibly know, but it was the dream.

He stared out over the sea again, watching the water turn to a frothy foam as waves furiously crashed to shore before drawing back out again. It reminded him how everything could change in a split second. Once the water came in and rushed back out, the shore was never the same. Each grain of sand in a different place than before.

The same could be said for this mission. If done right, his life could change drastically.

For the better.

Lochlan sat lost in thought for a moment more before he stood up and turned to look at Straik Castle.

It was a huge stone fortress surrounded by high cliffs and dark water on all sides. If Lochlan could own a stronghold as mighty as Straik, he'd be respected on both land and water.

This mission needed to be successful. Lochlan could not accept failure at any time, on any mission. But this one especially.

Straik Castle was owned by his good friend and fellow Amadán brother, Broderick MacLeod. They'd known each other for years and Broderick allowed him to anchor the *Hella* here when they needed to restock and catch up on the news of the land. Straik Castle was the only place Lochlan had ever called home.

Lochlan had Broderick to thank for introducing him into the world of the Amadán. Just as Thrash had recruited Lochlan to privateering, Broderick had recruited him into the Amadán.

"Good news, Cap'n?" Sam, his quartermaster asked, nodding at the letter clenched in his fist.

"Tell the men to ready the ship." Lochlan replied, ignoring the question. "We sail at dusk."

"So soon, Cap'n?" Sam groaned. "We just got here. I havena even had me a wench yet."

"Aye," Lochlan said, his tone tight as he answered his quartermaster, not in the mood to defend his decision to anyone, let alone Sam. It was unusual for Sam to question his authority, but the man, even though he hadn't had womanly pleasures yet, was a little in his cups, so Lochlan would let it go.

"Aye, aye, Cap'n." Sam said, his words slurring. He must have sensed Lochlan's unyielding tone so he didn't argue and instead the burly man sauntered off toward the castle to gather his men, grunting a greeting at Broderick as he approached.

"New mission?" Broderick asked, looking at the missive in Lochlan's hand.

Lochlan nodded. "Aye. We leave tonight."

"Already?" Beside him, Broderick sighed. "Ye havena been here long."

"I canna delay. This calls for me to sail to the English border. To Solway Firth."

His friend knitted his blond brows. "Ye'll need to get clearance. Even if ye're between our lands, they'll not take kindly to ye sailing in there."

"I know I *should* do that."

"But ye're not going to, are ye?"

Lochlan laughed, shaking his head. "I'll have to drop anchor in neutral waters and row in before making my way inland."

"Do I want to know?" Broderick asked.

"Nay, ye dinna," Lochlan answered honestly and looked up at the sky. Clouds were moving in, turning the sky an angry gray. The water would be rough. "'Tis naught for ye to worry about."

"Verra weel," his long-time friend clapped him on the back. "Come inside. Let's share some spirits before ye leave."

CHAPTER 3

*I*sobel still couldn't believe the situation she found herself in. But it would be a cold day in hell before she was forced to marry anyone. She would find a way out of it if it were the last thing she ever did.

She looked around at the men her father had assigned to escort her and her mother to her uncle's house in Seascale on the west coast. But first they were stopping in Flimby on an errand for James. The last thing Isobel wanted to do after what he'd just done, but she and her mother finally agreed so they could finally be free of him for a while.

The men were a pompous lot. All jewels and expensive clothes, their boots shined to perfection. They looked like they were attending a pageantry event, not protecting two women. If they were to be attacked, she had a better chance of protecting her and her mother than any of these fools did. And she would if she had to. Not that her mother couldn't take care of herself, because she could.

If there was one thing her mother insisted on, it was that Isobel could protect herself. But today, the usually cheerful Lady Anne looked forlorn and gloomy as she sat ramrod straight with her hands folded tightly in her lap. Her mother looked bone tired. The sway of the carriage had put her to sleep, and Isobel saw the deep sadness etched into the lines of her face. Not too long ago, they'd received news that her mother's brother had passed away.

They were traveling to pay their respects and to spend time with family that they had not seen for quite some time. Isobel was both dreading and excited about spending time with her uncle's wife and daughters. They'd been to court and visited the king, a distant relation to her mother and uncle. She wasn't accustomed to their ways, but was intrigued by their adventures all the same.

James had stayed behind to tend to business that needed his immediate attention. More than likely to pay off his debts now that he had received the payment for her hand in marriage from her future husband. She didn't miss his absence. She was thankful for the time away from him.

Her father was a cruel man. For reasons she could not understand, he loathed her very presence. She'd always attributed his rage toward her based on the simple fact that she was a girl. She served him no purpose. He wanted a son, and since her mother bore no children after her, he was stuck with his only child being a daughter.

Not a proper heir.

Their parting words kept replaying in her mind. She heard the exchange over and over.

Something about it gnawed at her. There were things her mother wasn't telling her. She wanted to know what those things were and the reason for the secrecy.

The men ahead halted, and their party came to a stop, pulling her from her dismal thoughts.

"What is it?" Lady Anne yelled to Sir John, their lead escort, awakened by their sudden standstill.

He trotted his horse beside their carriage. "A brief check of the proximity, my lady. Naught to worry about."

She nodded and turned to Isobel. "I don't want you to worry about what's waiting for you when we return."

Tears threatened, but Isobel held them back. She needed to be strong. Her mother was dealing with enough right now. So, instead, she dipped her head in agreement and watched the men as they scanned their surroundings, a little spark of hope igniting in her belly, but it quickly extinguished. James had already received the money, there was naught her mother could do to right the situation.

After a few minutes, she began to wonder why they were still stopped, even though they were traveling on a well-known path. Isobel thought the men were overly cautious since there had been no reports of trouble in this area for some time. But she supposed they could never be too safe. So she leaned her head against the cushion at the back of her seat and tried to relax for the first time since they'd begun their journey.

"My lady, we're clear to continue," Sir John stated and motioned for their party to start moving again. He glanced at Isobel but said nothing.

She'd long suspected that Sir John held an attraction of her. The thought made her shiver. A union between them would be most unpleasant. He was far too old for her, though that was quite common. He was so stiff and proper. His body didn't contain one fun bone in it, and his sense of humor was nonexistent. At least he wasn't the betrothed her father spoke about.

But she had no idea who her betrothed was, and that was very worrisome.

Her mother thanked him as he closed the door and the carriage jolted forward, wanting to get moving since the journey to Seascale would take at least two days. Two long, uncomfortable, boring days. It couldn't be helped, but it would give Isobel plenty of time to think about her situation and to develop a plan of her own. So Isobel figured she better settle in and get comfortable.

She disliked traveling. There was no other way to say it, and, under normal circumstances, she'd much rather stay home. But this time, she was glad they were on the road. Being in the same room with her father—the same home even, was—not something she wanted to endure right now.

She was so upset and angry she could have strangled her father with her bare hands. Her mother had said she'd deal with it, but Isobel knew better. If her mother could have stopped the union from moving forward, that would have been done already.

Isobel would take her circumstances into her own hands.

Perhaps she'd be asked to go to court with her cousins if they were asked to attend while they visited. If that were to happen, her father couldn't defy a royal order, could he?

CHAPTER 4

*L*ochlan and a few of his men watched quietly as the small traveling party passed by. They'd been tracking them for a while, and Lochlan couldn't help but smile.

This mission was going to be easier than he had anticipated.

The guards were useless. His hounds could protect the women better than these men. They were too busy talking to one another, using a cloth to pat the sweat from their brow, and drinking from skins to notice anyone lurking about. Either they were purposely ignorant or truly had no idea of their surroundings and the dangers the forest held.

Whatever the reason was, they had no business guarding the stables, much less two innocent women. Whoever had hired them was a damned fool. Or was it all part of Willys's plan? If it was, the man who had hired him hadn't thought it through. Lochlan was there for a reason, and hurting the lass wasn't one of them. But what if they'd been set upon by someone other than him and his men lurking in these woods? Brigands, vagabonds, and thieves preyed on the weak every day. Considering the area, this party stuck out like no other.

The carriage alone reeked of money. More money than most common folk would see in a lifetime. And those horses, fine specimens they were. If anyone were to show up that was up to no good, they would definitely be set upon.

Lochlan was actually doing them a favor.

He released a low whistle to alert his men to follow him as he moved quickly through the trees. Their horses were where they had left them, ready and waiting. All they had to do was snatch the girl and race back to the *Hella*, pushing out to sea before anyone knew what happened.

The *Hella* was currently out in neutral waters, just over what would be considered Scottish waters. Lochlan hoped that was enough to keep them unnoticed and unbothered.

The plan was to get in front of the group and then cut them off at the upcoming turn in the road. Striking so swift and fast that the guards wouldn't know what hit them—this way, he hoped there would be less bloodshed. But from what he'd seen of these men, he figured they would surrender out of fear, handing the lass over to him with hardly any resistance. Lochlan wouldn't be surprised if the men pissed themselves during the ambush.

Sorry sods, they were.

His men made their way to the spot they'd previously scouted and decided upon, the soft rustle of the leaves masking their steps.

The sound of hooves pounding against the earth, dampened from the previous night's rain, had the hair on Lochlan's neck standing up. They were getting closer.

It wouldn't be long now, and he would be a much richer man. With land to call his own. He was so excited he could almost taste it. He could picture the stronghold he would build. It would rival Straik Castle, but with his own personal touch.

He moved forward just an inch, then looked at his men. "Ready?" he asked.

But he knew they were. His men were some of the deadliest men on the seas. Cutthroats, all of them. But they were well trained. And loyal. Even if something did go wrong, he trusted them to have his back. To follow the code that men of the sea lived and died by.

Beside him, Honey nodded, his blue eyes alight with anticipation as he licked his lips. As a fellow Amadán warrior, he lived for battle.

Lochlan ducked down low to not be seen through the trees as the carriage started to pass by, the oblivious guards none the wiser.

Taking a deep breath, he whispered to his men, "Wait for my signal. Sam," he nodded in the direction of his quartermaster, "take the guard on the right. Angus, the one on the left."

He scanned the road and listened to the thud of the horses' hooves coming closer and closer. It was time they make their move. He took one last look to make sure no one else was around—the last thing they needed was a surprise.

"Honey and I will take the carriage," he stated. "The rest of ye, take the remaining men. No matter what ye do, no harm can come to the women."

When all his men nodded in agreement, he turned back to the approaching party, his eyes once again watching the road. A slight breeze ruffled the leaves and blew a strand of hair across his forehead and into his eyes. He ignored it, still focused on the road. Blood pumped through his veins. He couldn't remember the last time he'd participated in a raid. At least not on land. Most of his fighting took place on the water nowadays.

A thrill raced through his body as it always did before a battle. A warm hum settled in. He was itching to get this done. To collect his reward and get started on his castle. Maybe even find himself a bonny lass to share it with.

He held his breath as the party came into view, then watched and waited. When the group had nearly passed them, Lochlan burst through the trees, shouting his war cry, *"Is mise dubh uisge!"* His men followed close on his heels.

The two men leading the traveling party—he refused to call them guards—fumbled around, seemingly stunned, before they finally came to their senses and reached for their swords.

But Lochlan's men were too fast. Sam and Angus lunged at them, knocking them off their horses and throwing them to the ground. A solid punch to their jaws, and they were each out cold.

That was way too easy.

His men were tying up those that remained when Lochlan heard a piercing scream coming from inside the carriage. He unsheathed his sword, and with a final check of his men, he nodded at Honey, and he yanked open the door and stepped aside, allowing Lochlan entry into the carriage.

Two women stared up at him. Mother and daughter. The girl he was supposed to take sat ramrod straight with her hands folded in her lap, her blue eyes round in fear, but a defiance shone in them, nonetheless. He liked that.

The older woman seemed to possess the same spirit. She pushed her daughter behind her with a small knife pointed at him. He couldn't help the evil smile that crossed his lips. He couldn't hurt her. Mayhap he could scare her into backing down. He loved a challenge, even a measly one.

"What is the meaning of this?" she spat.

Lochlan ignored her question, drawn back to the blue eyes, still round with panic, staring at him.

In one sudden move, he knocked the blade from the older woman's hand before she could even react. The sharpened metal thudded to the floor, and he kicked it out of reach.

Shock reflected in the mother's eyes and in the way her mouth opened slightly, but she composed herself, a steely calm coming over her features as she asked, "Have you any idea who I am?" She planted her hands on her hips, staring him down before she pointed to her daughter. "Who *we* are?"

"Aye. I do," he said, his attention completely focused on her daughter. He'd never seen such a stunning woman before. A natural beauty. He could drown in her eyes of ocean blue. And if she had that effect on him, he would have to be diligent around his crew to keep her safe. "'Tis why I'm here." He flashed her a wicked smile.

Upon hearing him talk, the older woman's eyes widened, and she shrunk back. "You're a Scot." She blanched, her words spoken with such contempt.

"Aye. I am."

"I guess what they say is true, then. You're all heathens. What do you want from us? Money? Our jewels? We'll give you what we have on us, and then we will be on our way. It would be unwise for you to hurt us. I am the king's cousin."

Lochlan lifted a brow. The king's cousin. That was information he hadn't known before.

She scrutinized him, from his head down to his toes, and if it weren't for the slight tremble of her hands, he might have believed she was not frightened in the least. But he knew better. Yet, he had to give her credit. She was a tough one. Grown men wouldn't dare stare at him the way she did right now. So he took a menacing step toward her, wanting to rattle her. To throw her off-balance.

His tactic worked, and she stepped back.

"While all that sounds tempting," he said, closing the

distance between them, enjoying watching her squirm. "I'm here for the lass."

The girl gasped, and all but pushed her mother out of the way. No longer cowering in fear, she looked as if she were ready to take on him and all of his men. Seems he'd struck a nerve. The lass had fire. A trait he found most attractive.

He heard Honey chuckle from his vantage point at the door of the carriage.

"My father said that this matter would wait until after we've paid our respects to my uncle."

Her voice wasn't as high as he expected. She didn't speak in the same sing-song lilt the wenches in the pubs usually did. That observation aside, her words sunk in. What the hell was she talking about?

"Whatever James told you was a lie," the older woman stated. "We have not yet come to an agreement."

The missive had told him to take the girl and hide her until he was contacted again, with strict instructions not to harm a single hair on either woman's head. He'd been offended by that. Just because he was a pirate didn't automatically mean he would mistreat a lady. That was not who he was. But now he was confused—something that didn't happen very often. What agreement was she talking about? James was the man who'd sent him the missive. Lochlan needed to figure out what the hell was going on, and fast.

But before he could question the woman again, Sam approached the carriage and popped his head in. "Cap'n, Honey. We need to make haste."

Lochlan dipped his head in acknowledgment and pinned his gaze on the lass. Leaning forward, he reached for her arm and used his body as a barrier between her and her mother.

The older woman pounded on his back, but he barely registered the impact of her small fists. While he understood why she was doing it, and he didn't blame her, it was fast becoming annoying. He whirled around and pierced her with his most fearsome glare. "My lady, please cease before ye make me force ye to stop." He'd tie her wrists if need be.

"No!" Isobel screamed and threw herself between them. "Please do not hurt my mother. I will go with you. Don't hurt anyone else."

Finally, a woman with some sense. Though he was loath to admit so, it did prick his pride a little to know she thought him capable of hurting a frail woman.

"Isobel," her mother shouted. "What are you doing, child?"

Isobel stabbed Lochlan with an icy glare and swung around to face her mother. "Father has promised me to this," she turned her eyes to him and looked him up and down with disgust before continuing, "man."

Promised to him? What the bloody hell was she talking about?

"Heathen," her mother corrected her, the haughtiness in her tone not lost on Lochlan as both women studied him. He almost felt uncomfortable under their scrutiny.

Almost.

But he found he kind of liked how Isobel, as her mother had called her, was sizing him up. It sent blood rushing straight to his cock. Bollocks, the last thing he needed now was to have to hide his tenting plaid whilst he tried to whisk her away from here and onto his ship.

"Yes, heathen," Isobel spat as she stood tall and straightened her petite shoulders as if resigning herself to her fate.

At no point in time had they ever discussed Isobel being promised to him. Maybe she was addlebrained because she wasn't making any sense. Was that why her father was trying to get rid of her? Was she too much for him to handle in her diminished mental state? He'd seen fathers do far worse things to their daughters than marry them off. But he would go along with her story and tell her whatever she wanted to hear to get her to leave this place without a fuss.

"Aye, yer father did task me with yer safety. And I canna see ye safe unless ye choose not to fight me. So when I go out the door, will ye come with me willingly?" Lochlan asked, holding his breath, waiting for her answer.

She hesitated a moment, so he nudged the carriage door open wider and jumped out, offering his hand for the lass to use as support. But still, she didn't move.

"Lass," he said, trying to break her trancelike state. "Are ye ready?"

Tears welled in her eyes, and she sucked in a few deep breaths before she composed herself and nodded.

Her mother grabbed her arm and pulled her backward, trying to push her daughter behind her, but Isobel stopped her with a mere shake of her head.

"I'll be all right, Mother. I promise. This *man*," she flinched at the word, "will not hurt me."

"I'm here to protect ye, lass." Lochlan looked at the older woman, his stare sincere. "Ye have my word, my lady. No harm will come to yer daughter."

"Your word means nothing to me. You will pay for this, one way or another. I'll see you hang in the gallows."

"Mother, please!" Isobel begged and moved toward him but stopped to look at the hand he offered her in support. She dismissed it with a shake of her head and used the other side of the carriage for balance.

Lochlan dropped his hand and backed up, yet still stood closely should she need any assistance. He realized he'd given her quite the fright and so she could be a little wobbly on her knees. She lifted her skirts as she climbed down the stairs, and Lochlan watched as she sucked in a gulp of air.

As soon as they walked away from the carriage, Sam replaced Honey's position this time, shutting the door in the older woman's face before she could step out. He held the door tight as she railed against it, beating on it, and screaming at them.

"You bloody maggots! I will not allow you to take my daughter! I'll hunt you down and cut your bollocks off!"

"Are the men dead? How about Sir John?" Isobel asked, concern clear in her blue eyes as her gaze darted back and forth between the men who'd been escorting her and Lochlan's crew.

"They all still breathe," Lochlan said as he surveyed the work his men had done. As ordered, no one had been killed or maimed.

Bruised? Aye. But naught that wouldn't heal in due time. "Follow me," he ordered, and he moved in the direction of the woods where his horse waited.

"What will happen to my mother?" she asked behind him, planting her feet and refusing to go any farther until he answered her.

He turned to face her and was once again struck by her fair beauty. "No harm will come to yer mother. She'll be left with yer men to continue to their destination." He closed the distance between them and, with a tug of her arm, got her moving in the direction of the trees and out of earshot of the others.

"I may be promised to you," she said and yanked her arm away from him. "But that does not mean that you can drag me around like one of your animals."

He hadn't meant to manhandle her. He didn't want their conversation being overheard. The last thing he needed was for her men to learn of their destination. Pompous arses or not, he didn't want them to go to the king and bring an army down upon his head. Her mother surely would. She would stop at nothing to get her daughter back. Of that, he was sure.

He didn't want to make it easy for her. And he still needed to solve the mystery of why Isobel thought she was promised to him. He'd enjoy being the one she was promised to, but alas, 'twasn't him. There was some lucky laird over the border, waiting to possess this bonny lass—at least that was what James had said in the information he'd provided to Lochlan.

"Wait," Isobel cried, digging her heels into the dirt. "You have most of my men tied up." She pointed at the men lying on the ground, including her lead escort, who she referred to as Sir John. "And the others sleep. What if my mother is set upon by thieves and has no one to protect her? I cannot allow that."

Isobel looked back at the carriage once more. "I will not go a step farther until I know my mother is well protected."

Lochlan sighed. "Lass, I need ye to trust me. We dinna have a lot of time to dawdle. We must be on our way."

"I beg your pardon, but how am I supposed to trust you?" she said, her chin raised in defiance. "After what you've done. Your word is not enough."

Lochlan blew out a breath of frustration. He wasn't used to answering to anyone. Especially not a woman. But if he didn't reassure her, they wouldn't be going anywhere unless he threw her over his shoulder and forced her to go.

"My quartermaster will untie all the men." He nodded to Sam to do as he'd promised. "There are a few others hidden in the woods that will stay behind until she is well on her way. No harm will come to her. I've said it before, but I'll say it again. Ye have my word."

She stared at him for a long moment before she spoke. "I can walk on my own. I don't need you tugging me about." She pushed past him and walked into the woods as if she knew where the horses were hidden.

"Suit yerself," he said and continued walking as a familiar

whistle sounded behind him. Sam must have finished untying the guards and called the men together so they could all hurry back to the *Hella*.

Lochlan wanted to be in the water by dusk. Once they set sail, the landlubbers wouldn't have a clue as to where they'd gone.

CHAPTER 5

*I*sobel sat quietly on the mare she'd been provided, the reins held tightly in her captor's—no, her future husband's—hands so she had no choice but to follow him, and as much as she loathed to admit it, she more than admired his broad shoulders and muscular back. With its muted blue and green pattern worn thin in some places, his tartan was unfamiliar to her. Not that she knew a lot about the Scots other than what she'd heard, which was nothing good. The stuff nightmares were made of. The stories she remembered made them seem like they were all vile heathens, creatures who ate little babes for fun.

Her father hadn't given her the name of her betrothed, so she didn't know what clan he belonged to or where they were going. Some clans were worse than others, she imagined.

So far, her betrothed was not what she'd imagined. Thank God. The picture running through her mind since her father made his announcement was of a pot-bellied, smelly, balding man with missing teeth and no manners. The thought made her shudder.

But, he was none of those things. He spent a lot of time in the sun, for his smooth skin was tanned to a beautiful bronze. It suited him. His honey-colored hair was unexpected as well. She'd pictured him with the same flaming-red hair his people were known for.

Funny, she should be terrified of this man. But for reasons she didn't understand, she wasn't. If anything, she felt a strong sense of calm washing over her, even with her impending, forced nuptials.

And his nearness was causing little butterflies to flit around in her belly. A feeling she hadn't experienced before.

At least she was thankful that he'd given her a mount. The thought of her having to sit in front of him, flush against his chest, gave her chills. The good kind.

It didn't make sense, what she felt for him.

Whatever his name was. It wasn't fair. He knew her name, but only because her mother had blurted it out in front of him; although if the marriage contracts were already signed, he'd known exactly who she was before he ever came to get her. Yet, she knew nothing about him. Even his men were tight-lipped, only ever calling him "captain."

The sound of the sea echoed from a distance, and the faint smell of salt tickled her senses. She'd always loved the coast, but her mother disliked the water and preferred to stay inland.

They continued at a hurried pace, the crash of the waves growing louder and louder until at last the ocean came into view. Such an incredible sight. Sandy shores soaked up the water as it lapped toward them.

The horses came to a halt at the water's edge and her future husband dismounted. He reached forward and grabbed her about the waist, causing a chill to rush through her. He seemed to hold her right in midair for longer than necessary before he finally set her down and steadied her as her feet sank into the sand. He let out a high-pitched whistle, and within moments, a small boat manned by a single figure appeared from around the corner of a cove.

As the boat neared the shore, the men waded out into the water, steadying it from the waves bobbing it up and down as it fought to break free from the men's grips. Once they had it under control, they nodded to her betrothed and waited. After a quick nod toward his men, he stepped into the water and held out his hand, waiting for her to accept it.

Isobel liked the water. From a distance. She didn't want to be in it. He pushed his hand toward her again, and she shook her head, feet planted.

"Come on, lass. We must go."

She shook her head again. "Where is your castle?"

His face shadowed. "I dinna have one."

"What do you mean, you do not have one?" Isobel asked. That calm she'd felt earlier was becoming a sinking feeling in the pit of her stomach. Why would her father make a pact with a man that did not own a castle?

She wanted to throw up. If she got in that boat, who knows what would happen to her or where she would end up? But there was no way not to go because if she tried to run, he'd catch her. Or one of his men would.

She was trapped.

"Just what I said, lass. Now come here, take my hand. We need to leave," he commanded with a gentle urgency.

None of this made sense. He didn't have a castle. But how could he not? He was a laird, or that was what she had assumed. Her father had said he was a landowner, right? Had he been lying? Or was she mistaken? Because if this man didn't have a holding, how was their match going to protect the lands between them? It wouldn't be advantageous.

Moreover, if their lands abutted each other, why were

they heading out to sea? Her stomach sank. "I'm not getting in that boat."

"Ye will." He advanced on her, drawing near. "Willingly or not. If I have to throw ye over my shoulder, I will."

His blue eyes bored into hers, and she knew he was telling the truth. But she couldn't bring herself to agree. Fresh tears stung her eyes. How could her father do this to her? Had this ruffian lied about who he was? Or had her father known all along that he wouldn't make an advantageous match and set out to be rid of her? Did she truly mean nothing to him? She knew he could be cruel at times, but this betrayal broke her heart into a thousand tiny pieces.

"You wouldn't dare."

"Aye, I would," he said, and, without hesitation, the beast bent down and scooped her up as if she weighed no more than a feather and roughly tossed her over his broad shoulder.

"Set me down, you animal!" she gasped as she kicked her feet and pummeled his back. But it was useless. There was no way he was putting her down. And even if he did, what would she do? Really, what *could* she do? She had no idea where she was, and even less of an idea how to get back to her mother if he allowed her to. Which of course, by the feel of his tight grip around her middle as he carried her over his shoulder, he had no intention of doing. At least she had a nice view of his arse as he moved swiftly to the boat, her extra weight not affecting him at all.

And a nice arse it was.

Not that she would admit that to him. The bloody heathen.

He stepped into the boat, and she squealed when he seemed to teeter here and there, trying to regain his footing and balance the boat. All she could see was the two of them toppling into the water together, but the next thing she knew, he dropped her onto a wooden seat and ordered his men to paddle.

Isobel seethed as her stomach lurched. She'd never been in a water vessel before. She couldn't jump. She didn't know how to swim, and she was sure that these men would catch her quickly if she attempted to. If she didn't drown first. That was more likely.

To make matters worse, the farther they rowed away from shore, the weirder she felt. Her stomach started to revolt. Sweat dampened her brow. She felt sick, dizzy. What was happening?

"Ye're looking a little green, lass," her betrothed said. "Have ye ne'er been on a boat afore?" He seemed genuinely concerned. But she didn't care about his concern at the moment.

"No, I have not."

"Och, is yer stomach churning?"

"Yes," she said, but barely got the word out before she started to dry heave. He jumped up and grabbed her around the waist and pushed her to her knees, so she could get sick over the side of the boat. He even held her hair.

"There, lass. Once we get to the *Hella*, ye can rest. It takes some time to get used to being on the sea."

The *Hella*. What in God's name was a Hella? Maybe she didn't want to know. It didn't sound good. Sounded frightful. But she couldn't help herself. She had to ask.

"What is a Hella?" she croaked and leaned her head over the side of the boat again. The contents of her stomach were all but gone as she heaved once more.

"Instead of telling ye," he said. "I will show ye."

He beamed with pride as they steered the boat around the other side of the cove and a massive ship came into view. She couldn't believe her eyes. It was a tremendous size. Dwarfing any merchant ship she'd ever seen. Not that she'd ever been on one, but those didn't seem nearly as big as the one looming in front of her right now. The weathered wood was almost black. The mast jutted out as if angry against the darkening sky. There were men on board, and Isobel watched them as they lined up against the rails.

Was this a pirate ship? Was her betrothed a pirate? No, it couldn't be.

He couldn't be.

He was too kind. Compassionate. Well, minus the capturing her part. He saw to her safety, even held her hair while she got sick.

Pirates plundered and murdered people. Yet, she couldn't shake the sinking feeling in the pit of her stomach. The sight of the ship made her shiver, and she pulled her shawl tighter around her shoulders.

Her questions were answered as she saw a dark blue flag raised high. Its tattered edges a testament to its many days spent at sea. She narrowed her eyes to see the symbol embroidered on the material. Was that a skull? With a dagger through its socket?

Her heart raced.

What had her father thought when he'd made this arrangement? She knew he disliked her headstrong ways, even though her mother was the same way. But she'd never expected this.

The small boat slid along the side of the ship, bumping it softly. And then strong hands grasped her around the waist as her betrothed hoisted her up into the arms of another man and onto the huge monstrosity. She yelped at the unexpected move and the unwanted hands touching her.

All around her, men stopped what they were doing and stared. Stared, really. The attention made her uncomfortable.

"Welcome back, Cap'n," an older man with weathered skin said as Isobel sighed with relief as she watched her betrothed pull himself over the side of the boat and onto the deck. "I see yer mission was successful."

His gaze landed on Isobel, but he didn't greet her. Just acted like she was property that had been acquired during a raid. She might as well not be there, though he saw her sure enough as his leering eyes never left her bosom. So rude.

"She can stay with me if ye like," the older man said. His lecherous smile revealed two missing teeth.

Isobel shrunk back in horror. Surely, he wouldn't allow that. Would he?

Her betrothed narrowed his eyes. "The lass will be staying with me. In my cabin."

"I most certainly will not!" Isobel exclaimed.

A buzz rumbled amongst the men.

In one swift move, her brutish betrothed picked her up and tossed her over his shoulder, his strong arm bracing the back of her legs so she couldn't kick out. She'd only known this man for a short time, and she'd found herself in this position more times than she would ever admit to. It was mortifying.

Hoots and hollers rose from the crowd. Isabel's face turned beet-red at the lewd remarks they were shouting at them. She wasn't entirely ignorant in the ways of men and women, but some of the things they said made her blush even deeper. They couldn't possibly be true. She wanted to crawl in a hole and disappear. Or die of embarrassment.

She slapped at his back, trying to get him to put her down because having her in this position was adding more fuel to the fire, and they were being peppered with even more disgusting comments. But it did no good. "I have two perfectly capable legs," Isobel shouted, still pummeling his back. "That allow me to walk just fine, you savage."

"Aye, 'perfect legs' is a true statement." One strong hand

smoothed her dress down her leg, and she stiffened at the intimacy.

They descended a set of stairs and were instantly enveloped in murky darkness, only broken up by the shifting flames of a few well-placed lanterns. He paused in front of a door and gently set her back on her two feet.

She fisted her hands at her sides. "Do not do that again," she warned.

He grunted beside her, not concerned at all by her ranting. He didn't say anything else as he pushed open the door and stood aside, waiting for her to enter.

The room was black as midnight. No way was she going in there. Who knows what awaited her? She shook her head.

"Ye either stay in here or out there with my men. The choice is yers."

"You would give me to your men?" Her stomach lurched, the realization of her situation sinking in. "Does the sanctity of our arrangement mean nothing to you?"

"Lass, I've no idea what ye are yammering on about. I'm insulted ye'd think I would do such a thing." He grabbed her by the arm and tossed her inside, closing the door behind them.

Isobel stood stiffly as he lit a lantern, and the room illuminated. It was larger than she'd expected. The corners were still basked in darkness, but she noticed a writing desk set against one wall, a wash basin against another, and a large bed on the other side of the room. Her pulse quickened at the sight.

On the far wall, a small window overlooked the sea. She felt the sway of the boat, and once more she started to feel clammy, dizzy. It was only a matter of time before she was sick again, and before she could suck in a deep breath to ease her hammering heart, nausea overtook her, and she rushed over to the basin and heaved. The action was painful as nothing was left in her stomach.

He chuckled behind her and offered her a cloth to wipe her face. "Ye havena yer sea legs yet." He poured her a cup of water and handed it to her. "Dinna fash, ye'll get them soon enough."

She took a sip of the warm water, immediately feeling the sickening pull of her stomach once again, so she dipped the cloth into the water and wiped her face.

"Thank you."

Above and around them, she heard the footsteps of the men moving about, tending to their duties. "Your men, they call you 'Captain.'"

"Aye."

"You own this ship?"

He nodded, a smile spreading across his handsome face. "I do. Her name's the *Hella*," he said proudly. "She's my home on the sea."

She sank into a nearby chair. "My father promised me to a sea merchant." She refused to say he was a pirate.

Beside her, the brute chuckled. "A sea merchant?" He shook his head, and a honeyed lock fell into his face, and she watched as he swept it back with a swift move of his hand. "I'm no merchant, love. A mercenary, aye. A pirate, aye. But no merchant am I."

Her eyes widened. She couldn't deny it any longer. "Pirate? You're a pirate. That's unlawful. My father would not have agreed to a marriage arrangement with a pirate. You lied to him."

Stormy blue eyes narrowed on her. "A liar, I am no', I can assure ye."

"How else would you explain this...this..." she threw her hands out, waving them in the air, "situation?"

"Lass, ye are daft. Ye've not been promised to me, but," his gaze traveled over her from head to toe, "I wouldna have minded. Whoever he is that ye are promised to, well then, he's a lucky man."

"If you are not the one that I'm to marry, then who are you?"

"My name is Lochlan MacLean." He bowed low as if in greeting. "But ye can call me Chaos."

CHAPTER 6

*T*he lass's eyes were the color of the early morning sky, widening when he spoke his nickname.

He hadn't meant to frighten her, but he needed to rein her in somehow. If she kept running over him with her sharp tongue and strong attitude, his men would lose all respect for him. He'd look like a sod, being brought to his knees by a mere slip of a woman.

Lochlan couldn't have that.

Isobel sputtered. "Your name is Chaos?"

"Aye." He bowed in front of her again, dipping low and sweeping out his arm. "At yer service, my lady."

"Whatever in God's name did you do to warrant such a name?" she questioned, her teeth worrying her lower lip. A very rosy pink, very full bottom lip that looked soft and ripe for kissing.

"Some stories are best left unsaid." He tossed her a devilish grin and winked. He wasn't about to tell her how he got his nickname or how he became a pirate. Some things were private, and on a need-to-know basis, and she didn't need to know. At least not yet. That was in the past, and that was where it was going to stay.

"I know 'tis been a trying day for ye, but I need ye to listen to me, lass. If ye listen to nothing else I say, listen to this. Ye are no' to leave this cabin. Ever. Unless the ship is on fire, ye must stay put. Do ye understand? 'Tis for yer own safety. My men know better than to harm a lass, but I dinna want to take any chances. Ye only open the door to Honey or me. No one else. No matter what ye're told."

"I'm not safe?" she questioned. Concern paled her pretty face and he saw fear swim in the depths of her eyes. Knowing she was upset made his heart do a little flip—an unknown feeling. He didn't want her to be scared, but she had to stay vigilant, or she could be hurt. Or worse.

"You are my betrothed. Why would you bring me some-place unsafe?" Her bottom lip was dark pink and puffy. He wanted to take it into his mouth and taste it.

"As I've stated had ye been listening, we are not betrothed. I dinna know where ye get such a daft idea."

"You said my father hired you."

"Aye. I'm a mercenary. Lots of people hire me."

"Before my mother and I left to pay our respects to my uncle, my father and I argued."

"I'm sorry to hear that, but that has naught to do with me."

"You don't understand." She paced the room, smoothing the folds of her green gown with the palms of her hands. "He promised me to a Scottish laird. You."

Lochlan shook his head. The lass was severely misin-formed. "Ye were never promised to me as a wife." His gaze roved over her. "Though, I wouldna protest to the arrange-ment. Ye're quite bonny, lass."

Confusion marred her features, and pink tinged her

cheeks. "But, if you are not to be my husband, who are you? Why am I here?"

He chuckled. "Ye did come along willingly," he reminded her.

"I thought you were the man I was supposed to marry, coming to fetch me early!"

"Nay. I've no need for a wife. I'm married to the sea." What would his life look like if he married Isobel? She'd be a spirited partner, passionate in the bedroom he was sure. He could see her greeting him, her belly round with their bairn.

As that thought formed in his head, the ship lurched violently, throwing Isobel onto the bed.

She sprang up as if it scorched her, tilting her chin defiantly. "I need to go. Take me back to the shore." Her voice was stronger than she looked. The ship rocked again, and she steadied herself with a petite hand placed against the wooden wall, her pink cheeks losing their color again.

Noises from up above had them both looking to the ceiling. Something was amiss.

"I'm needed above deck. Stay here," he ordered.

"I will not."

"My lady, it wasna a request. This is the only place I can warrant yer safety. Lock the door behind me and dinna open it for anyone but me or Honey."

He left the room and paused outside the door until he heard the lock click into place, then he took the steps two at a time to see what was happening.

"Cap'n!" Sam called. "We've got a storm rolling in strong and fast." He pointed north.

Lochlan skimmed the sky. Off in the distance, the clouds rolled angrily in the dark sky, lightning illuminating the water in a steady beat.

Honey approached. "'Tis going to be a rough one, Chaos."

"Furl the sails!" Lochlan ordered as he took his place at the helm, struggling to turn the wheel to change their course. Their best route would be to try to meet the storm head-on at its outer edge, sailing at an angle. The stern would bear the biggest impact of the rising waves. The *Hella* could take it. She'd been through much worse.

He worried about Isobel tucked away below deck. She was sick when the waters were calm. The next few hours were going to be rough, indeed. But there was nothing he could do to ease her comfort right now. Now was the time to see them safely through this storm, with as little damage as possible.

Thunder roared above them as the ship listed on the rough water. Members of his crew pulled and tightened ropes.

"Heave! Ho!" they chanted over and over again as they brought the *Hella* into the best possible position to face the storm.

Within minutes, the storm was raging all around them. Rain splattered Lochlan's face. The drops landed with such force, each one felt like a pin piercing his skin. He fought the wheel. The damned thing had a mind of its own.

Men armed with buckets planted themselves along the gunwale, holding tight to ropes so as not to go overboard but ready to bail the water if it started sloshing onto the ship.

"To the devil with ye!" Lochlan yelled as the ship lurched violently to the left. He used all his strength to right the wheel. Sea water sloshed over the sides, and men slid amidships, the strength of the waves too much for them to keep their grasps.

He continued to take on the storm at an angle, maneuvering the *Hella* with an expert skill he owed to Thrash. He'd have to thank Thrash the next time they crossed paths.

Without the expertise afforded to him by his pirate mentor, he had no doubt this storm would have been impossible to pass.

"Man overboard!" someone yelled, and Lochlan watched as Sam and Honey fought their way to starboard, the wind pushing them backward two steps for every one that they managed to move forward. Honey raised his hand to shield his eyes from the whipping rain as he searched the water. The world was dark around them.

It would be impossible to see a man in the water. The swells were too big. The rain acted as a sight barrier.

"Chaos!" Sam hollered to Lochlan. "I canna see him."

Honey shook his head. "Me either."

Duncan, their first mate, made his way to the other side, still holding on tightly, and carefully leaning over to peer into the black, murky water. The waves churned, their angry white caps obscuring their view and it was nearly impossible to see anything. He turned and met eyes with Lochlan and shook his head.

The man was gone.

Their code stated that they left no man behind, but this storm dictated otherwise. There was nothing anyone could do. Even if they turned around, the odds of them finding the deck hand were near nil.

Lochlan's heart ached. He hated to lose a man and knowing that the deck hand died doing what he loved was little consolation. He sent up a silent prayer. He would ensure the man's family received a mighty booty so they'd know how much Lochlan had valued his service. He didn't even know who it was yet, but it didn't matter.

They were a family. He took each loss personally.

He forced his attention back to the *Hella* and steering her and the rest of his men to safety. He wondered how the lass fared below. She must have heard their shouts over the thunder and driving rain and fierce wind.

If Isobel had managed to get control of her stomach, she surely had lost it again during this storm. The helm fought against his hands. He gripped it tightly, forcing the wheel to move in the direction he wanted it to.

It seemed like forever before they finally saw the other side of the squall.

In the distance, the black clouds rushed by, replaced by spots of dark blue sky, as it began to lighten up, and the storm moved on to wreak havoc elsewhere. Thank the heavens. He turned the wheel and headed to the left of where the clouds were breaking up, taking a deep breath because they were through the worst of it. He remained on course, traveling straight down the outer edge of the storm. While it would still be a rough ride, the danger was over.

As they came out on the other side, Lochlan let out a long breath, releasing the tension that had built up in his chest. They'd only lost one man, and though one was too many, it could have been much worse. The *Hella* seemed no worse for wear, but they'd have to inspect her for damage in the morning when the light of day would assist them.

Sam approached solemnly, sorrow etched in the lines of his forehead.

"Who was it?" Lochlan asked, bracing himself for the answer. He could tell by the anguished look on Sam's face that he wasn't going to like the answer.

"Gunny, Cap'n."

Lochlan sighed, a sick feeling burning in his gut. Gunny was a lad. He hadn't been on the *Hella* for very long. He had only a few sails under his belt, but he'd proven to be able-bodied and useful. Good help was hard to find, but Gunny was different. He had an eye for the cannons, a natural talent, and was trained to take over that position.

Indeed, his crew had suffered a great loss this night, and Lochlan would make sure his family was well paid for his sacrifice.

CHAPTER 7

*B*elow deck in the captain's quarters, Isobel sat on the bed, holding on to the corner post for dear life as the vessel jerked to and fro. She'd retched more than once, and if the boat didn't stop its violent rocking and shaking, she was quite sure she'd be retching some more. She didn't know how because there was nothing left to heave. Her stomach hurt, and her ribs were sore, and just when she didn't think she could take anymore, the movement of the ship noticeably slowed. Beyond the small window, she could see breaks in the night sky where stars began to shine through. At last, her prayers had been answered. She hadn't perished in the storm, drowning in the angry sea.

With her mind occupied with the weather, she hadn't had much time to think of what she'd learned about her betrothed. No. Not her betrothed. Her captor.

Undoubtedly, that was what he was. Whisking her off into the depths of the sea for what reason? She hadn't the faintest idea.

Chaos. She shivered at his name. What kind of brute had a name like that? He'd mentioned several times her father had hired him. Why? Her father had already arranged her marriage. So why would he hire someone to stop her from visiting her uncle and other family? It didn't make sense.

A sharp knock on the cabin door startled her out of her thoughts. "Isobel, 'tis me. Unlock the door."

She had the good intention to leave the knave locked out of his own quarters. It would serve him right.

"Isobel?" he said again. "Are ye all right, lass?"

Was that concern she heard lacing his voice? For a moment, she almost felt guilty but then remembered she was the captive in whatever this game was that he was played. She remained seated on the bed, and after listening to him repeatedly jerk the doorknob so hard he was about to rip the entire door from its frame, she figured it was time to answer him. "I'm fine."

"'Tis about time ye answered me, lass. Now open the door."

"No."

"Isobel." His deep voice ground out her name.

It was his own stupidity for leaving her in charge of the lock, and she had no desire to open the door. Gods be. He could be damned. It was a small victory, but a victory all the same.

She couldn't help but be a little proud of herself. She bested a pirate. Or wait, a mercenary. What was he again? Both of those wretched things? But her victory was short-lived when she heard metal clink against the lock, and her heart sank as the knob turned and the door opened.

"Why did you ask me to unlock the door when you had the key all along?"

He surveyed the contents of the room before his eyes settled on her, his honey-colored hair wet and plastered to his handsome face. "I wanted to see if I could trust ye." He walked to his wardrobe and fetched a dry tunic, and with one swift motion, he tugged the wet garment sticking to his skin over his head and tossed it into the corner. He paused and pierced her with an icy glare. "I learned I canna."

"You cannot trust *me?*" Isobel laughed. "That's delightful coming from the likes of you. If I am to stay in your quarters, you cannot be here, much less undress in here. It's not proper. Do you wish to ruin my reputation? Brand me a harlot? Is that your goal?"

While she was admonishing him, her eyes dropped to his muscular chest. She wasn't unfamiliar with the male anatomy, but she'd never been within reach. Her parents had tried to shelter her from such things. But his bare chest filled her with both trepidation and aching. A longing she'd never felt before. His skin was a beautiful bronze from long hours in the sun. His muscles, spectacular and broad. A scar of some sort marred the otherwise smooth skin on the left side of his chest.

A tingle of wanting awakened in her nether region and the unfamiliar feeling had her shifting her position on the bed.

Then she thought about where she was and hopped up to stand in the corner and silently watch as he pulled the dry tunic over his head, covering the skin that had set her nerves on fire. If he'd taken notice, he didn't react. She was thankful for that.

"I understand ye dinna trust me," he said. "Ye are a means to an end. Nothing more. I have no desire to ruin or even tarnish yer innocent reputation. Ye already have my word that no harm will come to ye. My word is my bond. Ye need to remember that."

He was right. She didn't have any other choice but to trust him, and so far, he hadn't hurt her. Humiliated her, yes. Scared her, yes. But physically, she was in the same shape she had been in the morning when she'd left with her mother for her uncle's residence.

He walked to the door and turned to her once again. "I'm glad ye fared the storm well and unharmed." His voice was softer than earlier when he spoke of trust. "I've things to tend to above deck, but I'm sure ye are in need of sustenance. I'll return with food and ale in due time." That was the last thing he said before he stepped out into the corridor, closing the door behind him.

She immediately felt the weight of his loss. She knew she shouldn't, but she did. The feeling was so intense all she could do was stare at the spot where he'd stood.

Had she detected disappointment in his voice? But why? They'd only known each other for a day. She wouldn't even call them acquaintances. They knew of each other. But no more than that.

So then, why did she find herself yearning for him? Wanting him to come back so she could talk to him again? To find out who he really was, not just the man who snatched her from her carriage. But the real him.

The pirate. The mercenary.

There was something wrong with her. She was promised to another stranger. She was in no position to find *this* stranger appealing, but she wanted to know everything about him, especially why he'd chosen the piracy path in the first place—and now was as good a time as any to find out. The room was warm, and she fanned herself, trying to cool her heated skin. Where should she start?

Now that the ship wasn't rocking violently, she made her way over to Lochlan's desk. She refused to call him Chaos, not until she knew exactly how he came about the name, and even then, mayhap not. The writing desk looked as if it was carved from an exotic wood she was unsure she'd seen before. It was well cared for. She ran her hand across its shiny, smooth surface. It was polished to a sheen with a matching chair fitted with a feather cushion to sit upon. Chaos may not hold land titles, but he wasn't without coin from what she could see.

The bed was piled high with furs and throws of the softest material, and pillows stuffed with feathers instead of pine needles were placed near the extravagant headboard. Everything was of fine quality.

She sat down at the desk and opened the top drawer, feeling a twinge of guilt. But that passed quickly. She wasn't normally one to peer into another's private belongings but wanted to know who her captor was. She might even find a clue as to why her father had hired him to abduct her. And since she was stuck here in this room, what else was there to do?

Inside the first drawer were a quill, inkwell, and some blank parchment. A block of red wax and a seal stamp sat in the corner. She picked up the seal and studied the pattern. From what she could tell in its backwards position, it was a hawk with a letter *C* grasped in its talons.

C.

For Chaos.

She wondered again what he must have done to gain such a frightful nickname. She closed the drawer and opened the next one. This contained a bundle of letters tied with twill. Her curiosity was piqued and she carefully untied the bow holding the messages together and studied each seal, looking for the familiar *W* of her father. She didn't see any that appeared to be from James so she retied the stack and moved on to the middle drawer.

This was where he kept his books. His financial records. A ledger lying in the drawer before her beckoned to be opened, but again, she hesitated. She plucked it out and rifled through the pages but clapped it shut before she could see anything. The urge to pry was strong, too strong, so she slammed the drawer shut and stood. His books were his business. At least that was what she kept telling herself, but she couldn't help but be curious. Her father had hired him, so was his payment listed on one of those lines? Had he written what the payment was for? In what way had they communicated? Was there a letter from her father in that stack of tied papers?

She bit her lower lip, fighting the temptation to go back into the drawer and read each of the letters in the bundle.

But she couldn't do that. She wouldn't. If she wanted answers, she would have to ask Lochlan. So, to get her mind off of her father and whatever deal he'd made with her captor, she decided to move on to his wardrobe. One could tell a lot about a person by the way they took care of their clothes.

Several tunics and a few pairs of breeches were neatly folded inside, as well as a plaid and tartan with the same pattern as the one he'd been wearing when he ambushed her traveling party. Underneath the plaid was an intricate armband. Curious, she picked it up, the weight hefty in her hand. It was heavier than she expected at first glance. And beautiful. If she had to guess, she'd say it was made out of bronze because some parts of the design had turned that odd shade of green where a polishing cloth couldn't quite get in there to clean it out.

"What in the bloody hell are ye doing?" Lochlan bellowed from behind her.

She gasped and turned to face him. As she did, the armband slipped from her hands and fell to the floor with a clang.

CHAPTER 8

*A*fter tending to the deck and breaking the solemn news about Gunny to his men, he'd taken some time to reflect on the conversation he'd had earlier with Isobel.

It bothered him that she hadn't willingly unlocked the door. That she didn't trust him. But why? Had he done something to make her fear him? Well, other than the obvious. Maybe she was being overly emotional. She was a woman, after all. That had to be it, because everything he'd done from the moment that she stepped out of the carriage was for her own good.

Even making her board his ship. She wouldn't be safe anywhere else. He had enemies. Bad men that wouldn't think twice about slitting her throat because they thought she might mean something to him.

Her feelings shouldn't matter to him but for some reason, they did. The only thing he could do was reassure her of his intentions. He hadn't forgotten she needed to eat. She'd been sick all day, so hopefully, by now, her stomach would be settled, and she could sup.

He stepped into the tiny galley and put together a small

plate of cheese and crusty bread, then grabbed a pitcher of ale. He nodded to the cook, then made his way to his quarters.

He wanted to make amends. Just because he had to hold her on his ship until her father made contact didn't mean her time here had to be miserable.

But when he opened the door to his room and found her rifling through the items in his wardrobe, he was furious. Men had lost hands for less. The last thing he needed was prying eyes. His cabin was his sanctuary. No one ever came here except for Honey, and on the rare occasion, Sam, and they would never look through his things. They wouldn't dare. Both men could be trusted.

They were loyal.

The same couldn't be said for Isobel. Not that he didn't understand her reasoning behind snooping through his things, for he did. She was curious to find out why her father had hired him. If truth be told, so was he since she seemed rather willing to come with him. But he was angry, nonetheless. His ledgers were in the desk drawer. There was information in them that could cause him trouble. Big trouble. It seemed he hadn't thought this situation through as well as he should have.

Now, what was he going to do? As much as he didn't like the idea, he would have to put the fear of God in her.

"I, uh," Isobel stuttered. "I'm sorry. I just—"

He set the tray and pitcher on the small table. "Ye just wanted to nose about in my things? I thought as a lady, ye would have better manners than that. Who is the heathen now?"

His remark must have hit a nerve because she stiffened and lifted her chin, a gesture he'd noticed she did when she was getting ready to stand her ground. "What did you expect me to do? You're holding me captive on this boat. I can't go anywhere."

He raised a brow at her remark. "Ye could jump into the water. Lots of places for ye to go from there. Truly, at the moment, I have a mind to toss ye overboard myself. Besides, ye seem to forget that ye offered to come with me. Came willingly, as I recall."

"A misunderstanding, and you well know it. Had I known who you were, I would have never come with you. I would have fought you every step of the way."

With a cluck of his tongue, he pierced her with a stare that had made others shrink back in fear. "That 'tis where ye are wrong, lass. One way or another, ye were always going to end up in this exact place."

To her benefit, she held strong. Other than the slight widening of her eyes, she showed no fear. She kept her chin jutted out as if daring him to say or do more. Oh, he wanted to do more, all right. He wanted to smack her well rounded arse and kiss her soundly. The lass had spunk.

He loved that trait in a woman.

He could imagine her curves under that expensive gown. Her creamy white skin. The globes of her breasts tipped with rosy-pink buds. The thoughts shot straight to his cock, and he grew hard.

Blast. This was not where he wanted this conversation heading. And he needed to get his lustful thoughts out of his head. She was a means to an end. A way to fulfill a dream. Nothing more.

But if that were true, then why was he reacting so strongly to her? She was to marry another. She was a lady. Not some wench he came across in a pub.

"I apologize. I shouldn't have pried." She bent to pick up what had fallen out of her hands when she'd spun around.

"Leave it," Lochlan commanded. "Aye, ye're right ye

shouldna have pried, but there is naught we can do about it now. What's done is done. Sit and eat. I'm sure ye're hungry. Ye havena eaten since our paths crossed."

She gave him a wide berth as he walked to his wardrobe and picked up the ancient arm wrap Isobel had dropped. He was sure she didn't realize the history behind the band and it wasn't something he wanted to share with her. He placed it back under his linens and closed the door.

After filling their cups with ale, he took a seat in the chair opposite her and watched as she eyed him warily.

"Are you going to eat?" she asked quietly and placed a small slice of bread on a wooden plate.

"Nay, I supped earlier," he lied. The lass was much too thin. She needed all the sustenance she could get, and he didn't want her feeling the need to share.

"The storm we had earlier?" she asked. "Are those a common occurrence?"

Lochlan shrugged. "We've our fair share of them."

"Aren't you afraid your ship is going to sink?"

"Och, she's seen and been through worse. She always makes it through."

"She?"

He studied her for a moment until he understood what she was asking. "All pirates name their ships after the fairer sex."

"Interesting."

Lochlan was certain that she thought that piece of information was anything but interesting. Yet, he knew what she was doing. Talking just to talk. Hoping his anger would diminish and he would forget what she'd been caught doing. And he did find his furor lessening, but his lust was raging harder than before. Mayhap he needed to do the same thing, anything to get his mind off her kissable, pink lips. So, he decided to ask her some questions.

Get some information to tuck away that might be of use to him later.

"Tell me about yer family."

She looked surprised at his question. "Whatever do you mean?" she asked, sipping her ale, and looking at him over the rim of the cup, her big, blue eyes drawing him in. Tearing a small piece of bread, she squeezed it between her fingers before popping it into her mouth.

Lochlan had never been jealous of anything like he was of that piece of bread right now. He couldn't stop staring at her lips. So soft and full, and the way her tongue darted out of her mouth to wet them. It was driving him to distraction. He could barely keep track of their conversation. She was oblivious to what she was doing to him.

"Yer mother," he stated. "She loves ye verra much."

He didn't doubt it for a second. It showed in the way she'd fiercely protected her daughter. Her feelings were etched on her face. That was the one thing Lochlan had longed for. A mother that gave a damn about him. He didn't even know if the woman was still alive. He doubted it.

"And I love her," Isobel said. "She, without the blessing of my father," her face pinched at the word, "raised me to be independent. Or as independent as a woman can be. They didn't force marriage on me." She took a long sip of ale. "I'd always been told the choice would be mine. Well, until recently when I was told a union had been arranged."

"It's not something ye want?"

Isobel shook her head vehemently. "Most definitely not." She averted her eyes from his imploring gaze. "My father and I have not always seen eye to eye. Though he left my mother to raise me to be my own person, he never really approved of my wild ways, as he called them."

He watched as she swallowed another sip of ale. Lochlan's

father was unknown to him. His mother had never revealed who the man was.

"My father always kept me at a distance," she continued, her voice somber. "I've never understood why. My mother did her best to keep the peace, but there were times when I would look at him, and there was such anger and hatred in his gaze as he looked upon me. I know he wanted a son. But Mother never bore him another child. He hates me for being a girl." She stood up quickly and walked to the far wall. "I don't want to talk about them anymore. I miss my mother dearly. The thought of what she is going through is almost too much to bear."

"Yer mother knows ye are not in harm's way."

"How?" she asked.

"My men made sure she understood."

"How?" she asked again. "Was she hurt? Did your men hurt her in any way?"

"Of course not. My men wouldna do such a thing. They assured her ye would be kept safe."

Isobel looked unsure but left her mother's condition alone to pursue another line of questioning.

"I still don't understand why I'm here. For what purpose?"

"I canna answer that. In due time the answer will reveal itself."

He wished he could give her the answers she sought. The look of defeat in her eyes was killing him. He didn't want to crush her spirit, but other than her father wanting to force her to marry, he truly didn't know why he'd been tasked with abducting her. But it tore at his heart that she had felt as abandoned by her father as he had felt with his own mother. Only her father chose to do it right in front of her. He couldn't decide which was worse.

She sighed, the corners of her mouth turned down. "I would like to retire. I'm very tired."

Lochlan stood. "Ye can have my bed, lass. I'll go elsewhere."

Relief showed blatantly on her face. He understood but wished Isobel felt comfortable with him. He would never do anything to harm her. That wasn't his way.

"I'll leave ye to yer rest." He'd go in search of his men for spirits and tales. Things to take his mind from the beautiful woman warming his bed.

CHAPTER 9

*T*he sun shone brightly through the small, round windows above the bed, bathing Isobel in a splash of warm light. She heard the sloshing of the water, which instead of making her violently ill as it had earlier in the day, had lulled her to sleep last night. Opening her eyes, she observed the room for the first time basked in daylight.

The wood was stained a beautiful reddish-brown, and brass fixtures decorated a wooden chest in the corner. She wondered what was in there, then pushed that thought from her mind. She didn't want a repeat of last night. There would be no peeking.

While she knew Lochlan had been upset with her, he reacted to her prying into his personal belongings better than she'd thought he would. She had been frozen with fear, praying he wouldn't have her flogged or worse. He was a pirate, for God's sake. He had a reputation to uphold, but he'd treated her better than her father when she'd done something wrong.

Instead of punishing her, he'd fed her. He hadn't locked her in a room with no provisions for a day to think about what she'd done. No, he'd sat with her and offered reassurance to her that everything would be well. She didn't know how it ever could be, but a small part of her was starting to trust him. He would see things put to rights.

Lying on her side, she burrowed into the furs. God, his bed was comfortable. Even more than hers back home. But that only made Isobel miss her mother more. Was she worrying herself sick? Or did she truly believe Lochlan's men when they assured her all was well? Was her mother looking for her or waiting for the time when she would be let go? She sighed and swiped at a tear. How long would that be? It seemed not even Lochlan knew, or if he did, he wasn't telling.

A gull cried somewhere nearby, probably looking for fish. The sway of the ship and the warmth of the blankets lulled her into a contented rest. She'd close her eyes for a few minutes more. She wasn't ready to face the day yet.

Isobel had no idea as to how much time had passed when she was woken by the sound of rummaging in the room. She squinted an eye open to see who it was, not surprised to see Lochlan searching for something in his wardrobe.

She watched his back, admiring the taut muscles that rippled with every movement. He'd removed his tunic, but had left on his trews, though they hung low on his waist.

Never having been with a man, she was almost certain the thoughts running through her mind were not pure. Lady Anne would not approve.

"I didna mean to wake ye."

She glanced up, and she was met with fierce blue eyes. Beautiful eyes that looked like the sky on a stormy day.

"You didn't," she lied.

He shrugged. "I tried to be quiet."

Moving to her side, she gazed past him into the wardrobe. "Did you find what you sought?"

"Nay. 'Tis fine. I must've misplaced it." He shut the doors and sat at the table. "Are ye hungry, lass?"

She should be scared of being alone with this man in his quarters. On his ship. No one here would help if things went awry. What if he decided to ravage her? He was too large for her to fight him off.

Who was she kidding? She had none of those feelings when he was near. If he wanted to hurt her, he'd had plenty of chances to do so already.

A faded tapestry hung above the table, its edges frayed with age, swaying slightly as the boat rocked along the sea. The intricate needlepoint depicted an angry sea monster rising out of the ocean, arms reaching and grasping for men thrown in the water from their sinking ship. Only the top of the vessel was visible above the waves.

"Lass?" Lochlan brought her attention back to him. "Ye should break yer fast."

Burrowing into the throws, she flipped over, her back facing him. "I don't feel like eating." And she didn't. The constant movement of the ship was becoming the norm, but oft times, her stomach still wanted to rebel and spill the contents within. The thought of food made her insides churn.

"Ye need to keep yer health. If ye dinna eat, ye'll lose yer strength."

Isobel sat up quickly, drawing the throw with her to cover herself, and pierced him with a glare. "What am I doing here? Yes, yes, I came willingly, being the daft woman I am. But what was your reasoning for being in the woods? For ambushing my mother and me?"

The sigh he let out was deep and full of exasperation. "Some things are better to hear from the person setting the plan in motion."

"I don't understand what that means." The man was infuriating.

He pushed back from the table, the wooden legs of the chair scraping against the worn wood floor of the cabin. Grabbing a small cask from the cabinet, he set two cups on the table, poured a small amount of clear liquid in one, and handed the cup to her. He filled the other with a generous serving and took a long pull. As he swallowed, his throat bobbed, a hiss escaping his full lips, and then he blew out a long breath through his teeth.

"Yer family history is yer own. I know naught of any issue ye may have, other than what ye've previously revealed."

"I didn't think we had any." She had a mind to ignore the drink. She had no idea what it was. Lochlan's face when he drank his first sip wasn't comforting. She sniffed the contents of the cup, and her stomach turned. "As I've stated before, my father and I had our differences. I was a constant disappointment."

"Ye could never be that," he said quietly, watching her intently.

She laughed. "I'm glad you think so. My father did not. He didn't approve of my independent will. He thought I was taking too long to find a suitable husband, even when I'd been told the choice was mine."

"Seems an odd arrangement."

"Yes, my parent's had a unique marriage. One I didn't and still don't understand. I believe there are things they are keeping from me, but I don't know what and the reason why."

"Sometimes we dinna discover until later their reasonings."

She nodded and twirled her cup in her hands, swirling the liquid inside.

"So, ye've never been married?" He looked surprised.

"No. None of the men introduced to me had ever piqued my interest." *Not like you.* "My father wanted a match that would make our families stronger. I wanted a match that would satisfy me intellectually and emotionally."

"Ye each had yer own reasonings, opposite of each other."

"Yes. He and Mother would argue often. I'd hear them at night. I hated that I was the reason for the strife between them." It pained her so. She didn't want to think that the problems they'd encountered were due to her, but she was quite sure that was the case.

Lochlan shrugged and refilled his cup. "I'm sure ye were not their only issue, lass."

She'd never been called "lass" before him. Every time the word escaped his lips, it wrapped her in a warm hug. It was an odd feeling. A feeling she was ashamed to admit she enjoyed.

"I beg to differ. My name was muttered quite often by my father." They were wandering off-topic. "That doesn't matter." She scooted back in the bed and rested against the gigantic carved headboard. "How does my relationship with my father lead me here?"

A honey brow lifted in question. "That's probably a question best asked of him the next time ye see him."

"And when, pray tell, will that be?"

Her captor looked flustered.

"I dinna have the answers ye seek. I was hired for a mission. 'Tis all I'm doing."

"A mission for what?" she cried, frustration oozing out of every pore of her being. "I'm not some piece in a game of chess."

Pinching his nose between his thumb and index finger, Lochlan inhaled deep. "'Tis not for me to say." Abruptly he yanked open the door but looked over his shoulder at her before leaving. "Get dressed. I can't have this conversation while ye're so..." His stormy eyes dipped to her breasts, hidden behind the throw she clenched in her fist, and walked out the door without finishing his sentence.

The pirate was frustrating! He'd mentioned earlier he was a mercenary for hire. Pirates pillaged. Mercenaries did what? Whatever they were hired to do?

Lochlan "Chaos" MacLean was not an easy man to read. He both terrified and thrilled her.

CHAPTER 10

*U*p on the main deck, Sam rambled on, his voice rising as he tried to make his point to Lochlan.

"Chaos," he said, his tone serious. "The men need time on land. They're getting restless."

Lochlan looked out over the water at the calm sea. A welcome sight after yesterday's storm. He knew what Sam was alluding to. His men were due an afternoon with wenches to lose themselves in and let loose. Usually, whenever they were on land, at least one night was spent in debauchery.

Not this last time. They were only inland for a specific purpose, and there was no time for sensual pleasures. The small group he'd handpicked for the mission to capture Isobel were only allowed to do what they needed and then head back to the *Hella*. The other men stayed onboard, watching the waters to make sure no trouble befell them.

The original plan when he'd anchored the *Hella* at Straik was to stay for a few days. Let his men relax. Drink and do whatever else they wanted while on land, but his mission to capture Isobel left them with no time for any of those things. They restocked and set sail.

He owed his men some time off the ship.

"I hear ye, Sam. Damn, man. Ye talk as much as a biddy." He took a sip of mead, wishing it were the fine gin he had stowed away in his quarters. He also wished he had climbed into bed with Isobel. He knew she'd make a fine lover. Her pale skin spoke of her high station.

He had no business thinking such thoughts.

His quartermaster continued, undeterred by his slight. "We're not that far out. We can dock in two days and allow the men to blow off some steam and lose themselves between a women's thighs before heading back out to sea to wait for further instructions." The man rapped his knuckles on the weathered wood. "Besides, we need to reward the crew for keeping their wits about them while having a lady on board."

Lochlan nodded. Having one of the fairer sex on board was often seen as a bad omen for the ship. He'd heard the murmurs of his men when the fierce storm had hit, blaming the lass for the weather that had come so suddenly.

All superstitions, of course, but his men believed plenty of them. Stopping inland for a couple of days would go a long way to making amends to the crew and allowing them to relax.

Pushing away from the railing, he approached his helmsman. "Head for Straik Castle. We'll dock for a day or two."

Shouts rose from his men. He hadn't realized how much they'd missed not being able to go inland on their last stop. Mayhap once there, he could find himself a wench to erase Isobel from his mind.

He had no idea how long it would be before Isobel's father contacted him once again. So far, communication had come as a missive. He'd never met the man in person. Isobel had hinted that he hadn't treated her kindly throughout her life.

The thought of anyone mistreating her made his blood boil. The fact that the person was her father made him irate. Her father was supposed to protect her, not cause her harm.

Lochlan thought of his part in this scheme that was mostly unknown to him. He knew the basics, not the specifics. What if her father was marrying her off to an old man that wanted her for nothing more than to impregnate her with an heir? Lochlan was a man for hire, but he had standards. When he spoke with Broderick, he'd question him to see if he'd heard of any impending marriages taking place near the border.

Isobel was independent. Strong-willed, with a mind of her own. What if the man she was to marry didn't like those traits in her? What if he felt the need to beat her into submission?

The thoughts made him sick. He was having a hard time separating the mission and Isobel.

He felt the tilt of the ship as it changed course, heading to his beloved Highlands. His friend would be more than happy to put him and his men up for a few days. Just long enough for his crewmen to fill their cups and satisfy their lusts.

Honey approached him and leaned against the rail, his back to the sea. "Ye look lost in yer thoughts."

"Aye."

He didn't say anything further, and his friend didn't pursue the subject. "Ye've made the men happy. They'll enjoy a couple of days off the water."

"Do ye want me to send a man ahead to let Laird MacLeod know of our impending arrival, Cap'n?" Sam approached them and asked.

"Aye, once we get closer, ye can send Left Eye over to make Broderick aware. Ensure he lets him know that we have a lass with us, and she will need a proper chamber setup. The least we can do after her being stuck on this ship with us these past days is make her as comfortable as possible while ye men run amok tupping whatever taps yer fancies."

"Aye, Cap'n," Sam said with a smile. "Will ye partake, or are ye planning on bedding the lass whose every move ye watch?" His quartermaster didn't wait for his answer before he walked away, joining his men at the helm, steering the boat to get them on the course to Straik as soon as possible.

Honey roared with laughter at Sam's daring remark and left Lochlan to his thoughts.

CHAPTER 11

*A*fter days that had seemed like weeks locked in Lochlan's quarters, Isobel was thrilled to walk on steady ground again. She was tempted to drop down and kiss the sand when she'd stepped off the ship. Her captor was right by her side. Stiff and on guard. Was he afraid she would try to run now that he didn't have the protection of the sea?

A fierce-looking Highlander greeted them on the beach. The two men clasped each other in an almost brotherly embrace before stepping apart and focusing their attentions on her.

She felt her skin heat and shifted from one foot to the other, uncomfortable with the scrutiny. She wasn't a prized hog gone to market. They shouldn't be studying her with looks on their faces that wondered how much she would fetch from the highest bidder.

Not one to show her true feelings, Isobel lifted her chin and stared the stranger dead in the eyes. Not saying a word.

"The lass has spunk, Chaos. She put up a fight?" They both laughed, and Isobel was affronted.

"I have nothing to put up a fight against, *sir*." She emphasized that last word, wanting them to know she would not be intimidated. She might not have learned what the plan was, but she would eventually, as she was curious to know what part her father played in the whole thing. And if her future husband was involved.

"I'm Broderick MacLeod, my lady." He bent into a small bow after his introduction. "It is lovely to meet ye." For a Scot, he had lovely manners. Mayhap she could convince Lochlan to leave her here.

Maybe he was the laird she was supposed to marry. He didn't appear to be a knave. Perhaps there was hope for her yet.

"Isobel Willys, my laird." She curtsied as if she were greeting the king and dipped her head slightly.

He offered her his elbow, and she slipped her hand into the warm crook of his arm as he led her from the shore to the path that would lead them to the castle looming in the distance. "I hope my friend has been treating ye as ye deserve. He can forget his manners at times."

Lochlan scoffed beside her.

She bit back a giggle as they continued along the walkway but said nothing.

Inside the castle, they entered the Great Hall, where a huge spread had been laid out. Broderick held out a high-backed chair for her and waited patiently as she sat down, then settled into the seat beside her. Lochlan pulled out the chair on her other side, but Broderick called him over to sit at his right side.

Lochlan looked over at her as if he didn't want to leave her alone, so close to his friend, but acquiesced and did as Broderick instructed.

Maids rushed over and filled their cups with ale, while others came forward with large platters overflowing with fragrant fares that tickled Isobel's senses. A maid offered a tray to Broderick first, but he leaned over to Isobel and asked her what foods looked good to her.

"All of them." She spoke the truth. After being on the ship for however long with only a limited variety of food options available to them, to have a platter piled high with such appetizing sustenance presented to her was like heaven.

Broderick grinned and filled her plate with a selection of meats and set it down in front of her. Ripping a small loaf of bread in two, he handed her half with a smile, revealing even, white teeth. Lochlan could learn a thing or two about manners from his friend.

"How long are ye staying?" Broderick directed his question to Lochlan, who was finishing the ale in his cup with one long swallow.

"A couple of days at the most. My men needed," he looked to Isobel and lowered his voice, "time with some wenches."

Isobel widened her eyes in shock but said nothing.

Broderick laughed. "And ye?"

Lochlan grimaced. "What about me?"

"Ye dinna need time with one of the local wenches?"

Isobel watched the men's exchange quietly. It looked as if her captor was getting flustered. Her knowledge of pirates was lacking, but she was quite sure bedding women was commonplace amongst them.

"I'm not here for that. This stop is strictly a boon for my crew. We'll be back in the water soon."

"Since when?" Broderick asked but didn't wait for an answer before turning his attention to her. "Isobel?" Broderick asked. "Have ye sailed often?"

Lochlan had the gall to guffaw at the question. Broderick slapped his friend heartily on the back.

"The lass doesna have any sea legs. She tossed her stomach more than once the first day or two."

She felt her cheeks heat and pushed back from the long

table. "If you'll excuse me, I think I'd like to rest." She shot a scathing look toward Lochlan. "On a bed that is stable and doesn't rock to and fro like a cradle for a babe."

With a whistle, Broderick stood up beside her. "Please, follow me. I'll take ye to Mary. She'll show ye to yer bedchamber and get ye settled for the night."

"Thank you for your kindness." She peered around him and pierced Lochlan with an icy glare. "Mayhap, you can teach your friend some of those manners."

Turning on her heel, she didn't wait for Broderick's direction. She headed toward the entrance of the Great Hall and smiled at the young woman that stepped forward.

"You must be Mary."

"I am, milady." She curtsied and grabbed a basket outside the door. "I'll get ye settled into yer room. The laird has picked a lovely chamber for ye. The fire is already flaming. It'll be nice and warm for ye." She paused and cocked her head to the side. "If ye'd like a bath, I can arrange that for ye as well."

A bath sounded divine. "I would love that, Mary. Thank you."

The woman nodded and led her up a circular stairway. "Of course. Once yer set, I'll fetch the bath water for ye."

A short time later, a tub was brought into the room, and buckets of water were carried in to fill it. Mary provided her with a bar of soap scented with herbs and left a drying cloth on a small stool she'd moved over.

"I'll be close by. If ye need me, call out."

"You're too kind. I can't thank you enough." She watched as the young woman gave a curtsy and shut the door behind her. She then stripped out of her clothing, which also needed a good washing. But it was the only gown she had since her chest of clothes was left with her mother when Lochlan whisked her away. She'd worry about that later.

Sinking into the water, she moaned at how wonderful it felt. She scrubbed her body from head to toe with the soapy herbs, washing away days of salty air, and then sat back and enjoyed the feel as the heat loosened her tired limbs.

Her mind drifted to her captor and the banter he and his friend shared. Whenever Broderick had paid any heed to her, Lochlan's gaze would darken, almost as if he were jealous.

She'd be lying to herself if she said that didn't fill her insides with warmth not due to the heated water.

A man had never shown jealousy for her before. But then, she'd never been in the position she was in now.

She could only hope the man her father promised her to would be as kind and handsome as Lochlan. But deep down, she doubted it would be so. And she was quite certain whoever it was would have a hard time living up to Lochlan's charms.

CHAPTER 12

*A*fter the meal had been cleared away, Lochlan and Broderick sat in front of the huge fireplace, drinking ale.

Broderick cleared his throat. "So, the lass. Is she the mission ye had to leave so abruptly for the last time I saw ye?"

"Aye." Lochlan emptied his cup and held it up to a maid passing by who stopped to refill it with more ale.

"Ye are a kidnapper now?"

"Hardly."

"'Tis what it appears to me."

"Shows how much ye know. I'm keeping her safe until her father reaches out."

Broderick lifted a brow in question but didn't say anything else.

"Have ye heard of any marriage agreements happening in the near future with the border families?"

Broderick laughed. "That's an odd and verra specific question, Chaos."

Lochlan shrugged. "Just curious. I've heard rumors. Wondered if ye'd heard the same."

"I'm assuming that the lass is in one of those rumors to be married?" Broderick's stare bored into him.

"The lass doesna want to be married."

"And ye're the one that sailed in for the rescue?"

He shook his head. "Not at all." He wished that were the case. The more days he spent with Isobel, the less he wanted to hand her over to her father when the time came. He understood their relationship wasn't a loving one, but he didn't understand the man's motive for having his daughter kidnapped. From what Lochlan had seen so far, the lass was willing to do what was expected of her. Was she happy about it? No. Nor would he be if he were in her situation.

Broderick kicked at a log on the fire, causing sparks to flare. "She hired ye?" He sounded surprised.

"Nay. 'Tis not like that." He stared into the flames leaping and stretching up toward the flue, looking for an escape. "Ye ever agreed to a mission and then change yer mind?"

His friend barked out a laugh, deep and boisterous. "Ye've fallen for the lass." He swallowed a long swig of ale and wiped his mouth with the back of his hand. "What do we always say before we go out?"

Lochlan grunted. "Never mix business and pleasure."

Broderick nodded dramatically. "And what have ye done?"

"Aye, I know. Ye dinna need to keep reminding me. This is different."

"How?"

Lochlan stood and began pacing in front of the fireplace. He had too much energy humming through his veins to sit still. All he wanted to do was march up to Isobel's bedchamber and lose himself for the night in her beauty and warmth.

If only that were an option. He pushed his fingers through his hair, scratching his scalp to clear his head.

"I dinna think the lass is getting a fair deal. Her father is using her as a pawn, but I havena figured out what for yet."

"Since when is our work fair? Oft times, it's the exact opposite. I think ye need a wench to clear yer head. Ye've been out to sea too long."

Lochlan shook his head. The very thought of taking a wench to bed felt like an insult to Isobel.

Then, a red-haired lass made eye contact, a welcoming smile revealing a missing side tooth. He sighed and shook his head. Any other day, he wouldn't have hesitated to take her to his bed. His time with the English lass had changed his thinking. The redhead pouted but moved on to another member of his crew who had no problem saying yes, and they wandered off together.

"Sit down, Brother, ye're making me nervous." Broderick waited until Lochlan sat and picked up his cup of ale and had a swallow. "What's this mission? Give all the details."

"On paper, 'tis quite simple. Kidnap the lass and keep her safe until her father makes contact, then deliver her to her father and future husband. Once completed I get coin and land to call home."

"What land? The lass is English. Is he giving ye land in England?"

He hadn't even thought about that piece. He'd assumed the land would be in Scotland. But would her father have access to Scottish lands to grant?

At the look on Lochlan's face, Broderick swore. "Come on, Chaos. How could ye have not thought that? Ye didn't ask what land ye would receive? That's sloppy."

He agreed. Lochlan had accepted this mission far too easily without thinking it through. In doing so, he went against everything he'd been taught. Study the situation. Ask questions. He'd been caught in a rare moment of self-reflection and had been blinded by the overly generous offer.

"Bloody hell." Lochlan stood up once again. "I need to go check on Isobel."

"The lass is fine."

He shot his friend a look, and Broderick put his hands up in defense. "Fine. Ye go check on yer woman."

Lochlan paused for a brief second as his friend's words sunk in. He would be honored if Isobel were his. It was a thought that had entered his mind almost every night since he'd first met her. But like the offered land, she too, was just a dream.

Stopping by the kitchens, he grabbed two cups and a tankard of ale and then took the stairs two at a time until he reached the hallway where Isobel had been given a room for their stay.

A maid exited a room, closing the door quietly behind her. He approached her. "Lady Isobel?" he asked. The woman pointed him to a chamber three doors down on the left, and he nodded his thanks.

At the door, he paused, taking a deep breath, unsure of why his skin was suddenly damp with sweat. He knocked softly and waited. He heard rustling and then steps coming to the door.

"Mary, I'm all—" The door swung open, and the sentence hung unfinished in the air between them. Her blue eyes were round in surprise. "Lochlan," she whispered. His name dripped like honey from her tongue.

He smiled and held up the cups and ale. "I thought ye could use a drink."

"I…" She looked down quickly and stepped behind the door, hiding her body from him, but not before he'd glimpsed the nightshift she wore. "It wouldn't be proper. I'm not dressed."

"Ye look perfectly fine to me."

She gasped. "One minute." She closed the door but didn't latch it. After some shuffling, she opened the door, and he noticed she'd wrapped herself in a long shawl, covering herself.

He tried not to let his disappointment show. The thought that she hadn't shut him out completely was a win in his eyes.

"Please, come in." She swept her arm out and stepped aside to allow him entry.

His chest swelled. He felt as if he'd just been given the keys to the kingdom. He stepped inside and set everything down on the table in the corner. "I hope ye're finding this room more to yer taste."

She remained standing by the door, her hand on the latch. "The room is fine, thank you. But there was nothing wrong with my quarters on the *Hella*. I found the space quite comfortable, other than the constant rocking."

Lochlan was surprised to hear her say that. He thought she hated being on the ship.

"Oh, don't get me wrong," she said, seemingly having read his mind. "Sea life is not for me. I prefer the stability of being on land."

Chuckling, he filled each cup and handed one to her. "They each have their high points." He took a sip, almost emptying the cup in one swallow. He was actually nervous sitting here in this room alone with her. A daft response since this wasn't the first time they'd been alone.

"How long do you plan on staying here?" she asked, settling onto the deep red chaise lounge with a yellow flower pattern stitched into the fabric.

"A few days at most. The men earned a night to themselves, and then we have to make some needed repairs to the *Hella* thanks to the storm." He frowned, thinking about all the tasks to be completed. "They shouldna take too long. Then we can be back on our way."

Sadness blanketed her face. He fought the urge to tell her it was going to work out fine in the end. But the words would be a lie since he didn't even believe them himself. Wetness rimmed her eyes, and his heart clenched. The last thing he wanted the lass to do was cry.

He stepped forward and enveloped her in his arms. To his surprise, she didn't refuse his offer and instead melded her body to his. She felt so wee compared to him as she clung to him and sobbed. His hand smoothed her flaxen hair. "There, lass, let it all out." It broke his heart to listen to the deep, wracking breaths she took. It hurt him even more that he was the cause for her pain.

"I'm sorry," she sniffled and looked up at him, her eyes exploring his. For what? Answers he couldn't provide. She laughed. "Look at me, sobbing like a girl."

"Nay. I think ye've had the weight of the world on yer shoulders recently, and everything is sinking in." He dipped his head and placed a kiss on her forehead, breathing in the herbal scent of her hair. She must've had a bath while he and Broderick had been talking. He should've done the same before coming in here. 'Twas the least he could do.

Burrowing her face in his chest as she held on to him, he bit back a curse. This was a bad idea. All he could think about was carrying her over to the large bed, laying her upon it, and worshiping her body until the sun dawned.

Isobel sniffed again and stepped back, breaking their connection. Instantly, Lochlan felt the cold emptiness in the space she'd just occupied. She sat down at the table and picked up her cup, twirling it in her slender fingers. He stood stock-still, afraid if he moved, he would scoop her up and kiss all her fears away.

"I know I've asked before, but mayhap you'll reconsider."

She took a sip of ale. He wanted to nip her neck as he watched her swallow. "What is my father's plan? I have no way to stop whatever has been put in motion. Would it cause so much harm for me to know what is coming, so I can prepare myself for the inevitable?"

CHAPTER 13

*I*sobel held her breath as she watched Lochlan wage some type of internal war with himself. Could he be feeling the same as her? The whole situation was wrong. But she couldn't help the emotions that roiled within her, igniting little flames of fire deep in her belly.

She didn't think he'd answer, but in one swift move, he was in front of her, on his knees. Looking vulnerable and distraught and oh, so handsome.

"My lady." He hadn't called her lass but by her proper moniker. She found she much preferred lass. "Never have I taken on a mission where I go back on my word. But I find this one most difficult. The reward promised doesna hold a flicker of a flame compared to ye."

His confession took Isobel by surprise. Was he saying what she thought he was? Was she not the only one with these awakening feelings?

"What is this mission you speak of?" she asked quietly, wanting to know the answer even as dread unfurled deep within her.

He clasped her hands in his warm, strong ones. "Yer father

contacted me. Said he would pay handsomely if I would accept the mission that he proposed," he admitted quietly.

She couldn't believe Lochlan was finally going to tell her what all of this was about. She gave a slight nod, urging him to continue.

"He told me ye and yer mother would be traveling to visit your family and pay respects to your uncle who had recently passed. I was to ambush ye and take ye away, careful that no harm came to either ye or yer mother."

"But why? I don't understand."

His thumb rubbed over her hand, the friction of heat sending sparks up her wrist and into her arm. "He believed ye were planning something to get yerself out of the marriage he'd arranged. He couldna have that. He needed the union to go through as promised." Lochlan kissed her palm.

"Lass, yer father has debts. Many debts that he canna possibly repay. He needs the coin that was promised to him for this union."

Isobel searched Lochlan's face, looking for a sign that he was lying. How could that be true? Her father could be cruel and unkind, but such a plan was unexpected behavior—even from him. He really had no concern if his actions caused her pain. Tears sprung in her eyes. "Are you saying my father was selling me to the highest bidder?"

A pained look crossed his face. "Aye."

She pulled her hands out of his grasp. "And you were helping him in this, this," she searched for the correct word, "this scheme."

"Twas before I met ye, lass." His stormy blue eyes clouded with emotion.

"You were going to help my father sell me to a man so he could pay off his debts?" She pushed him away and stood, walking briskly to the other side of the room.

"I didna have all the details. I didna understand the situation."

"And now you do?" she cried. "What changed?"

"Ye did. Ye changed everything." He stood and turned to her, his beautiful eyes pleading for understanding.

She shook her head, holding out her arm to stop his approach. She didn't want him to come any closer to her. Whenever he touched her, her feelings got mixed, making it difficult to sort out right and wrong. How could she possibly have feelings for a man that cared so little for her? But even as the question ran through her mind, she knew it wasn't true. He was a mercenary, yes. But a mercenary with a kind heart if that were even such a thing.

Since the first day they'd met, when he snatched her from her mother, he'd treated her with nothing but kindness and respect.

"Lass," he pleaded, taking a step forward.

"Don't." She moved to the door and opened it. "I would like you to leave."

"Please dinna do this, lass."

Refusing to meet his eyes because she knew she wouldn't be able to keep her composure, she kept her gaze to the floor. "Please go," she whispered.

Lochlan stood still for a few long moments, and she didn't think he would comply with her request—until he walked stiffly to the door and paused beside her.

"I would never hurt ye, lass." He bent and placed a soft kiss upon her head and walked out the door, not looking back as he descended the stairs at the end of the hall, his boots echoing on the stone.

A sob wracked her chest as Isobel shut the door and collapsed on the bed, tears flowing freely down her cheeks. Her mother drifted into her thoughts. She couldn't have known about her husband's plan. She would've never agreed to travel if she had.

Anne was a strong woman. Once she found out what James had done, she would unleash her wrath on him. Did she know about the debt? Perhaps. There was something going on between her parents. Was this arrangement the reason behind their strife? Isobel didn't think so.

She refused to believe that her mother would play a part in such a dastardly scheme.

But why this plan? Why now? She needed answers from her father.

Standing, she dropped the shawl she'd used to shield her from Lochlan's imploring eyes and grabbed the cup and tankard of ale he'd brought with him and carried them over to the bed. She poured herself a full cup and drank it quickly. A fit of coughs made her gasp for air, but she didn't care. She poured another cup full and drank deeply.

When the tankard was empty, she placed it and the cup on the table and wobbled over to the window, pushing aside the tapestry that kept the chilly night air out. She had a view of the sea from this room. Heard the waves crashing to shore in the distance. The gulls were circling, searching for fish, and diving into the water when one was spotted.

What would it be like to live a life out on the ocean? To not have to worry about the world happening inland?

She slid down the wall and sat on the cool stone floor. The bed beckoned, but her mind's eye kept portraying an image of her and Lochlan tangled in the throws. The image heated her skin and quickened her pulse.

Even after his betrayal, she still wanted him. The only thing she could do was ignore him. No matter how hard a task that would prove to be.

CHAPTER 14

Over the next two days, Isobel had refused to see Lochlan. Hell, she refused even to leave her chambers—she requested all her meals to be brought to her.

The only reason he knew Isobel still was there was through her maid, Mary. The woman wouldn't give him a lot of information, but enough to know that the lass was faring well.

The *Hella's* repairs had been completed, and their supplies had been restocked. They were ready to head back out to the water. He just needed to get Isobel to come out of her chambers and on the ship.

Even Broderick had tried talking to her with no luck. Surprising, since the lass seemed to fancy him over Lochlan. If only Broderick's wife, Maggie, were home. Her charm and strong personality would win Isobel over. But she was away visiting a friend.

He sent Mary up to tell Isobel that they needed to depart, bracing for the refusal he'd heard all too often over the last two days.

He was on the shore, watching the last of their provisions

being loaded onto the ship, when Broderick approached him, clapping him on the shoulder, as he stopped beside him.

"The lass has fire. I'll give her that."

Lochlan grunted. "Too much for her own good."

"Och, ye're too hard on the girl. She's had a rough week. How would ye feel if ye found out yer father had sold ye off so he could save his sorry arse?"

Lochlan sighed and pinched the bridge of his nose. "I know. The situation is less than desirable. I've tried to make it right. The stubborn lass willna listen." He was exasperated. Their time at Straik Castle had been distressing, to say the least.

"Ye need to turn on that Scottish charm that used to get ye all the wenches when we were younger," Broderick chuckled.

Honey laughed beside them. "That charm seemed to have left his body the first time Lady Isobel opened her mouth."

Lochlan swatted his friend's head. Because Honey was more than a crewman. He was a friend and confidant. He treated Honey almost as his equal, and that meant a lot. Lochlan's crew knew the same respect they gave to him was to be afforded to Honey.

"That's the last of the supplies, Cap'n," Sam hollered from the ship.

Lochlan nodded and looked past the *Hella* at the sea. The waters were choppy, but no storms seemed to be approaching. If they were to leave, now would be a perfect time. All that was left to do was convince Isobel.

Whistles sounded from his crew, and Lochlan followed their eyes to the path that led back to the castle and sucked in his breath.

Isobel, head held high, chin jutted out stubbornly, walked toward them. Her gown, a beautiful navy blue that rivaled the sea, fit her to perfection. A gown she hadn't possessed before.

Broderick laughed. "Close yer mouth, Chaos. Show some manners, man."

He snapped his mouth shut and shot a death glare to his friend. Gathering his wits, he walked up the path to meet Isobel and escort her the rest of the way to the ship. She kept her eyes straight forward as he approached, essentially ignoring him.

"Lass, ye look beautiful."

The compliment went unanswered as she stepped past him, leaving his extended hand empty, while she stopped in front of Broderick.

Sinking into a deep curtsy, she dipped her head. "Laird Broderick, thank you for your kindness and generosity. The gowns you've provided are lovely. I'll be sure you are compensated somehow once I arrive home. I apologize so much time was spent in my chambers. My manners were severely lacking. I hope if we meet again, the circumstances will be different."

Broderick bowed and placed a soft kiss on her hand. Lochlan felt as if he'd been sucker punched. How he wished she'd bestow that kindness upon him. If he were anyone else, he thought she might.

His friend assisted her across the beach and to the ship, helping her keep her balance as she walked up the gangway and onto the deck.

He fought the urge to punch something, namely Broderick. His fists clenched at his sides. The anger came from someplace deep within him.

Broderick held up his hands in defense when he returned. "Easy, Chaos. The lass is all yers. Ye need to figure out how to get over this stumbling block ye find yerselves in. Dinna fash. She'll come around. I've no doubt."

Lochlan turned, feeling guilty at his misplaced anger but unable to control it. He climbed the gangway and waited for the rest of his crew to board.

"Raise anchor!" he called and took his place at the helm and directed the *Hella* out to deeper water. Out of the corner of his eye, he saw Isobel make her way down to his quarters, two crew members carrying a chest following at her heels. More gifts from Broderick, he assumed.

He was anxious for her father to make contact. The bastard had no idea what he was getting himself into. Lochlan sure as hell wasn't going to turn over Isobel to his or anyone else's care. He'd fight for her 'til the death. But he knew his men. Knew his ship. The only death that would be seen would be James Willys's. He would pay dearly for the hurt he'd put his daughter through.

Later, once they were in the open water, land nowhere near, he knocked on the door of his room and waited, surprised that Isobel opened the door.

"May I come in, lass?"

She shrugged but stepped back, allowing him entry.

"Can we talk?" He hadn't walked farther than the doorway. He was trying to give her space, though it pained him. All he wanted to do was wrap her in his arms and promise her everything was okay. He'd promise her the world.

"Seems ye may have grown yer sea legs after all," he stated, noting that she didn't look ill or pale.

Nodding, she wrapped her arms around herself. "My stomach seems to have settled. The rocking isn't bothersome anymore."

"That's good." He ran his hands through his hair. "Lass, I know ye were given a lot of hurtful information at Straik, and I apologize for that." Her blue eyes focused on him, boring into him, and he felt them pierce his very soul. "I want ye to know that I have no intention of going through with whatever plan yer father has for ye."

"But what of your promised coins and land?" She asked, confusion clouding her eyes.

"There will be plenty more opportunities for me to acquire what I seek. I dinna feel yer life should be bargained for those items."

Her petite shoulders sank in relief.

"'Tis not right what he is doing. Ye deserve so much better than whatever awful life he has planned for ye."

"How will you stop him? He won't let it go. And you won't receive your land."

He sighed. "I was blinded by the land offering. Who knows where this land is or even how much it is. Against my usual response, I heard land and thought it would be in Scotland and enough to make a home. But why would yer father have land in Scotland to give away? If he had land, it would be in England. And I dinna want to live in England. No offense," he said with a smirk.

"My mother has spoken of land in Scotland in the past. I don't think it is still in the family holdings, but I can't be certain. So it's all about the land? That's what you are about?"

"No!" he growled. "Afore? Yes. But not now." He wanted to punch the wall in frustration. "I'm not doing a verra good job of explaining myself. I couldna care less about the land. The coin. All of it. The only thing I care about is ye."

Her eyes rounded in surprise. "Me?"

"Aye, lass. Ye." He closed the distance between them. "From the moment I opened that carriage door and laid eyes upon ye, I had doubts I couldna go through with this mission." He dropped to his knees in front of her and buried his face in her lap, the folds of her gown soft against his skin. "I want ye, lass. I want to protect ye. To keep ye safe from harm. I vow that I'll never let anyone hurt ye. Ye have naught to fear when I'm with ye."

She lifted his head in her small hands, their heat warming his heart, and her ocean-blue eyes showed such promise. When she dipped her head and brought her lips tentatively to his, he nearly lost his mind. He wrapped her in his arms and held her tight. He wanted so much more. To lay her out on the bed and show her all the pleasures of the body. To make her forget the predicament that they now found themselves in.

"Cap'n!"

"Chaos!" Shouts came from outside his quarters. Crewmen yelling his name.

Something wasn't right.

Isobel grasped his shoulders. "What's wrong?" she asked, her voice laced with fear.

"I dinna know, lass." They called his name again. He went into his wardrobe and grabbed his sword and a dirk, shoving it into the cuff of his boot. "Stay here. Lock the door behind me. Only open it for me. Understand?" At her nod, he pressed a kiss to her lips and ran out the door. This time, he didn't wait to see if she locked it behind him.

Honey met him on the steps leading to the deck.

"What's going on?"

"A ship approaches starboard. English."

He held out his hand, and Sam passed him the spyglass. Looking through, he searched the sea until he saw the vessel fast approaching. It wasn't pirates. It appeared to be a merchant ship. What business did they have with the *Hella*?

"What do ye make of it, Cap'n?"

"I'm not sure. Ready the men in case. Have the cannons ready to fire." For a flitting moment, Gunny crossed his mind, but he didn't have time to think about his lost crewman.

Sam, showing how strong he was in the position of quartermaster, barked out commands. The cannons aimed at the oncoming ship, ready for battle if needed. His crew stood at the guardrails, swords drawn.

Lochlan couldn't be prouder. They line up, waiting, as welcoming as Hades. He couldn't have assembled a scarier-looking crew if he'd tried. Each man would give his life to protect the *Hella*. He would never be able to thank them enough.

He peered through the spyglass again, watching their approach. They'd be here within minutes. He scanned the length of the vessel, searching for clues as to their intent. Suddenly, a white flag was raised.

"Cowards," he muttered under his breath. How could they surrender before his crew even challenged them?

"That was unexpected. What's yer plan?" asked Honey, standing tall next to Lochlan, his fingers wrapped around the hilt of his sword.

"Chaos?" Sam asked.

Lochlan knew they were waiting for the order to stand down. He didn't give it. Let the bastards approach while pissing their breeches.

Two men climbed into a boat that had been lowered into the water. One of them took up a pair of oars and steadied the vessel as another man clumsily followed behind them, sitting ramrod straight as one more man, rotund in nature, joined them and plopped down with a thud. None of them spoke as they rowed toward the *Hella*.

One leg planted on the rail, Lochlan waited, unmoving, staring the group of men down as they came closer. When they were nearly at the ship, one of the men who wasn't rowing—an older man, Lochlan noted—lifted himself and shakily stood. His arms out as he tried to balance himself while he greeted Lochlan's crew.

"Please, I'm not armed." He carefully patted his clothing and slowly twisted to prove his point. Lochlan was unsure he'd know how to wield a sword even if he were armed. "I'm looking for the mercenary pirate called Chaos."

"Ye've found him. What do ye want?" He assessed the four men. Definitely not pirates. It was apparent the one asking for him had not spent a lot of time on the water, if any at all. The other man, similar in age to the one speaking, sat quietly, watching him with narrowed eyes.

"May we board?"

"What's yer business?"

"I believe ye have my wife on board," said the man with narrowed eyes, puffing out his already hefty chest.

Was the first man Isobel's father? He saw no resemblance. And the fool with him? That was who he had promised his daughter to? The man was a drunkard. From this distance, Lochlan could tell the man enjoyed his ale too much, his bulbous nose and red face signs. Along with the slight slur to his speech. Money or no', the man wouldn't know what to do with a lass as fine as Isobel. He couldn't give her what she needed or craved.

What she deserved.

"Are you Chaos?" the man sitting down called out.

An Englishman, Lochlan determined from his accent.

"We've had communications. You're expecting me."

Lochlan considered turning them away. But he wanted to know what kind of man sold his daughter to the devil to save his arse.

"Let them aboard," he ordered and stepped back from the rail, waiting for the men to be brought up on deck.

He crossed his arms as he watched the two scramble up the side and studied them as they stood before him. He towered over both men. The one he assumed to be Isobel's father looked at him nervously. The other eyed him with disdain.

Lowlanders. He thought to himself.

"Sir, is my daughter safe?"

Lochlan ignored the question. "James Willys, I presume?"

"Yes, yes." He bobbed his dark head up and down. Isobel's looks did not favor her father in the least. "Where is my daughter? I'd like to see her."

"The lass is fine."

"Good, good." James had an irritating way of repeating things.

"I'm here to take her home."

Lochlan pierced the Scot with a warning look to step back. "And ye are?"

"Her husband," the man spat. "Now, go fetch her. We need to be on our way."

"The lass is unmarried, and she is not a dog. I will not be fetching her as ye so stupidly commanded."

"Ye better watch yer words, pirate. As soon as we step on land, we'll be married." He tucked one hand into the overly vast waistline of his breeches, while his other hand smoothed down one of the few strands of hair he had left on his balding head.

Lochlan had the urge to smash the man's pudgy face into the deck. This cretin was who Willys thought was worthy of his daughter? The father was just as much of a fool as the Scot he'd made a deal with.

A rustle of murmurs emitted from his crew, and all eyes focused behind him.

"Father?"

"Bloody hell!" Lochlan cursed at the sound of Isobel's voice.

CHAPTER 15

*I*sobel took in the scene before her. Her father was standing on the deck, talking to Lochlan, along with someone she didn't recognize. All of Lochlan's crew looked as if they were teetering on edge, ready to attack at the drop of a pin.

"My dear Isobel," her father crooned and moved to approach her.

Her father had never called her by endearments. She drew closer to Lochlan and intertwined her fingers with his. He closed his hand around hers tightly in reassurance, and she breathed a sigh of relief. He wasn't going to let anything happen to her.

James watched the move, and his face turned an angry red. "Step away from him this instant." He took a step toward them but retreated at the deadly look on Lochlan's face.

"I believe the lass has made a decision."

The unfamiliar man with her father came forward, not taking heed of the terrifying look Lochlan gave him. "'Tis not the lass's decision. I've paid for her. She belongs to me."

She couldn't stop the gasp from escaping her mouth, yet she stood tall. "I belong to no one."

"Ye stupid wench. Yer father and I have a deal. It's already been agreed upon." He waved his arm in her father's direction. "I paid for ye. Yer father paid off his debts. Ye come home with me. Bear me lads and lassies, and all will be well."

"I will do no such thing," she spat. The man was vile. As he spoke, she could see the gaps in his gums where his teeth were missing. His overall appearance, from his girthy belly to his balding pate, was revolting. What was her father thinking? He must be daft.

"Isobel," her father spoke up, throwing a warning glance at the man he'd made a deal with. "We talked about this before you and your mother left, and—"

"And you had me kidnapped!" She cut him off before he could finish his sentence. "Stowed away on a ship with some stranger until you could hand me off to another stranger. Do you have no bounds to how far you will go?"

Lochlan laid a strong hand on her shoulder, gently rubbing her tense muscles. He dipped his head and whispered in her ear, "Easy, lass. Ye've made yer point. Let me do the rest." He edged her behind the protection of his back and rested his hand on the hilt of his sword.

"Ye both need to get off my ship."

"Not without my wife."

"She's not yer wife. Nor will she ever be." Lochlan glared at the men. "I dinna usually give people more than one chance to exit their way off my ship. But, since I care for Isobel deeply and ye are her father, I'll make an exception and say it again. Get off my ship. Or my men will help ye off."

She couldn't see her father's face from her stance behind Lochlan. She could only feel the taut muscles of his back tensed and ready for a fight as she splayed her hands there.

For her.

He was doing this for her.

She'd never felt so cherished.

Before she knew what was happening, Lochlan pushed her away and raised his sword as her betrothed—the thought of which made her want to hurl—lunged himself at Lochlan with a knife raised high in his meaty hand. A mixed look of shock and pain crossed his face as the blade of Lochlan's sword sank into his beefy gut. The man turned his eyes on her as blood trickled from the corner of his mouth before slumping to the wooden planks of the deck.

"What have you done?" James hollered, looking between the man on the deck and Lochlan. Blood pooled around the crumpled figure. He wouldn't be rising again.

"I protected yer daughter, as I swore to her I would. Something ye should've done as her father instead of selling her off like chattel."

She watched silently, waiting for her father to explain his actions. He didn't. He sputtered, looking flustered as he seemed to search for the words to say. He pinned his eyes on her, standing a few feet behind Lochlan. His steely black stare narrowed in anger.

"You daft girl. Are you this stupid? You're no better than your mother. Falling in love with the first person who shows you kindness."

"Father?"

He shook his head, looking around madly at the men surrounding him. "You've ruined everything. Without this union, you've ruined your mother's life."

"I've done no such thing. Mother did not agree to this match. This was all something you concocted behind our backs. For what reason?"

He was backing away from Lochlan, moving closer to the guardrail. "You need to be married. You're too old to still be at home. I needed you gone."

His words went through her like a hot knife. Stabbing her with every word he stated.

"Father."

"I'm not your damned father! Can you not see that?"

What was he talking about? He'd raised her.

"Your mother was a whore. I saved her a lifetime of embarrassment by marrying her. Now you've gone and messed everything up."

"How dare you speak of Mother that way."

"Or what? You'll get your distant relative, the king, to help you? Are you daft? Don't you realize he's the reason your mother and I even married? Why I raised you as my own?"

Isobel tried to comprehend all of the information he was shouting at her with such venom in his voice.

"Every year I received a payment from court. Coin to make up for the sacrifices I made for you and your mother, who had acted stupidly and found herself unmarried and with child.

"No one else would have her. You were both lucky I offered to save her reputation and your future of not being raised as a bastard child."

Tears streamed down Isobel's face as her father—no James—continued spewing his hate filled explanation.

"Your mother kept filling your head with fantasies of being able to choose your husband and your future. That was fine until the money stopped. I was certain by the age of twenty-two you would be married. A union was long past due. But you kept refusing. And then the money stopped. Our debts grew."

"Never once did you mention our finances were poor."

"Would that have changed your mind and made you marry?"

Isobel worried her bottom lip with her teeth. She

honestly couldn't say that knowing that information would have forced her to take a husband.

"Just as I thought. We couldn't sell our house, we needed a place to live. None of this would have happened if you'd only done what was expected of you."

"What of your own debts? All the coin you lost gambling?" She nodded at James's look of surprise. "Yes, I heard you and mother fighting into the early hours of morning many times." Lochlan's hand squeezed her shoulder in reassurance. It felt nice to have his support. It helped her stand strong against the man who'd just admitted he never did care for her. Or her mother for that matter.

"I was able to pay my debts until recently, when I hit an unlucky streak."

"You lost my dowry." Her words came out in a whisper as she pieced everything together. "Did mother know?"

James didn't answer her questions.

"You did, didn't you? That's why you needed to sell me to the highest bidder. You'd be rid of me and have your debts paid off."

"Isobel," Lochlan said, his voice low. "I think enough has been said for now."

She shook her fist at James. "You'll pay for your scheming. I'll make sure of it."

"Isobel," Lochlan repeated. "Go below deck. James and I are going to talk."

"I'm not going anywhere." She heard Lochlan sigh heavily behind her, but he didn't ask her to leave again.

Instead, he walked over to the side of the ship where the rowboat floated and called down to the two men waiting. "Go back to yer ship. Ye've no further business here."

"Not without Lord Willys."

"If ye want to see yer ship again, ye'd be smart to leave. Now."

Lochlan's voice sounded ominous. Deadly. She even noticed some of the color drain from James's face.

Moments later Isobel heard the splash of water from the oars as the boat returned to its ship.

"Are ye okay?" Lochlan asked, stepping in front of her.

She nodded and gave him a small smile. "I have a better understanding of why things were the way they were." She pierced James with an icy glare. "You will pay for everything you've done. I'll see to it. Mother will see to it."

James scoffed at her threat.

"You'll have no home to return to."

"You stupid girl," James spat.

Within the matter of a second, Lochlan was in front of James, bunching the material of his shirt in his fists, forcing the man she'd always called Father to look at him, his face fierce. Lochlan's eyes were dark with anger, the color swirling like a stormy sea.

"Ye watch yer tongue when speaking to Isobel," Lochlan ground out.

All the color drained from James's puffy face as his eyes darted back and forth from Lochlan to Isobel.

James bobbed his head up and down and Lochlan released him.

Slowly, James edged toward the rail, backing away from them.

"I should have known you'd ruin everything in the end." James focused on Isobel as he spoke scathingly. "You and your mother are exactly alike." He looked at Lochlan, hatred in his eyes, before turning to Isobel and addressing her again. "Whores. The both of you."

In one swift move, he climbed over the guardrail and toppled into the water.

"No!" Isobel yelled, running over to the side of the ship, and looking into the dark water. She couldn't see him.

"Lochlan!" she cried, sobs erupting from her chest as she searched the area where James had fallen. "I don't see him," she sniffled. "I don't know why I'm crying. He doesn't deserve my tears."

Lochlan wrapped her in his arms and hugged her tight. "Och, lass. Ye've had a trying day." He smoothed her hair as she cried into his chest.

"He doesn't know how to swim."

"I know, lass. I fear that was his intention."

It all made sense now. Her father's hatred toward her. The late-night arguments between him and her mother. Why she and her father had no shared traits.

Because he wasn't her father.

The discovery was a shock.

Isobel needed to speak with her mother. She was sure her mother had her reasons, but Isobel wanted to understand the background and the why.

The crewmen looked at them and shook their heads.

"He didna surface, Cap'n."

She felt Lochlan sigh and he dipped his head to hers.

"I'm sorry, lass."

CHAPTER 16

*T*wo days later, the *Hella* anchored in familiar waters. Broderick and his wife, Maggie, were waiting on the shore as he and Isobel came up. He lifted her easily around the waist, careful not to get her feet wet, and placed her on the sand with a smile.

It had been a rough couple of days for Isobel. She'd shed many tears as she rehashed every year of her life and realized how her father truly wasn't her father at all.

"Chaos." Maggie greeted him with outstretched arms.

He bent and kissed her on the cheek. "Maggie. Ye look lovely." He approached his friend and then clasped Broderick's hand in his and gave it a healthy shake.

Isobel stood back, waiting for them to finish their greeting, and he reddened. "Och, where are my manners? Maggie, ye and Isobel havena met yet. Ye were away the last time we visited."

"Aye, I was, but I've heard lots about ye, Lady Isobel," she said with a small curtsy.

"Oh, please, no formalities. I'm just Isobel. And I, too, have heard much about you." The two women hugged.

"Well then, let us leave the men to themselves to do whatever men do, and get to know each other. Ye must be hungry." Maggie was still talking as the two women walked through the sand and up the path that would lead them to Straik.

"So, I see ye still have the lass," Broderick remarked, a knowing smirk on his face.

"Ye would have done the same thing in my situation. Her father was a fool."

"Was?" Broderick asked as they watched Lochlan's crew come ashore.

"Aye. 'Twould be a miracle of the gods if he still breathed."

"Ye killed him?"

"Nay. I didna have to. The bastard killed himself when he jumped off the *Hella* into the sea without knowing how to swim. Now, her betrothed. That was a different story. I did kill him," he stated proudly. "Death could not have happened to a better person."

Broderick clapped him on the shoulder. "Ye know I want to hear all about it. Let's get something to drink, and ye can tell me about the past sennight's adventures."

They followed the women to the castle and entered the Great Hall, where they were met by serving wenches with cups full of ale.

"He tracked ye down in the open water?" Broderick asked once they finally settled down.

"Aye. I made no secret that we were headed north. All he had to do was ask around and he would know where to find us. I'm no' sure how they caught us so quickly, but they were sailing as if the devil himself was on their tail."

"And Isobel? She looked to be faring well."

Lochlan shrugged. "She's had a rough few days. Finding out the man she knew to be her father wasna has been difficult for her."

Broderick shook his head in disbelief. "I canna imagine how hurt she must have been at such a betrayal."

Isobel caught Lochlan's attention as she passed the entrance to the Great Hall and moved toward the stairs that would bring her to the chambers set up for her. She must be tired after such an ordeal. He had the urge to follow her and offer his comfort.

Beside him, Broderick whistled low, and when Lochlan turned to him, his friend gave him a knowing smile.

"Does she know how ye feel?" He asked, dipping his head in the direction where Isobel disappeared to go to her room.

"Aye. Somewhat. Mayhap."

Broderick raised a brow in question. "Pardon?"

"'Tis complicated."

"How so?"

"I've shown her with my actions. Letting the bastard that she was sold to know that he would not be laying a hand on her as long as I breathed. And when he challenged, I did no' hesitate to strike him down. I told her I would always protect her. No harm will come to her when she's with me."

"'Tis a start, I suppose," Broderick jested. "And she for ye?"

Lochlan shrugged. "I believe she feels the same. Her kisses are filled with passion, and she comes into my arms as no other woman afore."

"Have ye bedded her?" Broderick asked.

"Nay, 'twasn't the right time or place on the *Hella*. She was mourning the life she knew. The man she thought she knew. I didna want to take advantage of that."

"And now?"

Lochlan sighed. "Now? Now I canna get the thought of her out of my mind."

Broderick laughed. "What are ye waiting for then? Go see yer woman. We can catch up anytime."

His friend stood up and stretched, then walked toward

the kitchens, leaving Lochlan sitting alone, giving him no company he could use to prolong going to see Isobel.

"Bastard," Lochlan muttered. Broderick was always trying to play matchmaker.

Unfortunately, he knew his friend was right. He couldn't delay this further.

'Twas time. They needed to talk. To see if their minds were in the same place.

~

Lochlan paused outside the door of Isobel's chamber, hand poised to knock, but he couldn't get himself to follow through with the gesture.

He dropped his hand and retreated a few steps, pacing the floor.

What the hell was he supposed to say? What if she rejected him? He pinched the bridge of his nose with his thumb and index finger and inhaled a deep breath.

No one paid him much attention as he walked back and forth talking, under his breath, preparing himself for all possible scenarios—but only one would bring him joy.

Approaching her door once again and hesitated. Mayhap she was resting, and he should wait until later after they'd had their final meal with some ale. He could really use some right now.

The door swung open before he could turn around and make his way back to the Great Hall. Maggie stepped out into the hall, her eyes landing on Lochlan and her mouth turning up in a knowing smile. She poked her head back into the room.

"Ye've got a visitor. I'll send up the bathwater shortly."

Well, that decided for him. He couldn't possibly turn

around and run now, could he? The thought crossed his mind. Nay, he couldn't. He exhaled loudly, and rapped his knuckles on the wood, and waited, even though the door was already partly open.

Isobel appeared in front of him, her cheeks flushed pink.

"Lochlan." His name dropped into the air as a breathy whisper.

He straightened his shoulders and cleared his throat. "I, um, I ..." What the hell was wrong with him? He was acting like a lad. "Can we talk?" He finally asked.

He held his breath as he waited for her to answer and breathed a sigh of relief when she stood back and waved an outstretched arm, welcoming him into the room.

Maggie had assigned her one of the bigger, more elegant rooms. Tapestries, new by the stiff looks of them, hung on the stone walls. A large four-poster bed was in the center of the far wall. Furs piled high provided plenty of coziness. He would rather be the source of her heat. He could keep her plenty warm wrapped in his arms, surrounding her body with his.

He dragged his eyes away from the bed. He had to get the images out of his mind of her writhing beneath him as he brought her to pleasure.

On the table, a pitcher of ale and cups had been placed there recently, judging from the full belly of the pitcher.

Isobel followed his eyes and wiped her palms on her gown before clasping them together. "Would you like some ale?" She entwined her fingers.

It looked as if she didn't know what to do with her hands.

He could think of something and nearly groaned aloud at the thought.

"Aye, please," he answered.

He watched her hands shake as she poured the ale into

two cups and set the pitcher back on the table. She handed him the cup, and he accepted it with a "thank ye."

"Is the room to yer liking?" He wanted to punch himself, making nonsense small talk to skirt around the issue.

"Yes, it's quite nice." She sat in the stuffed chair set by the fireplace. "Maggie and Broderick have been nothing but kind."

He nodded. The long space of quietness between them lingered and felt like an eternity. Why was this so awkward?

"Lochlan."

"Isobel."

They both chose that time to start talking.

"My apologies, lass. Ye go ahead."

Her pink tongue licked her lips nervously as she inhaled in a hiss. She caught her lower lip between her teeth and nibbled.

He almost threw his head back and moaned. Those lips. Beautiful. Red and swollen from her worrying them with her teeth.

He wanted to kiss her and not let her go.

"Would you like to sit?" She asked.

"Nay, thank ye. I'll stand."

She dipped her head and he couldn't take the edgy, stilted conversation any longer. He dropped to his knees in front of her and enveloped one of her soft hands in his. His large hands dwarfed hers.

"Isobel," he stated again. This time, he would not back down from the topic. "Ye've been through a lot since we..." his words trailed before he continued, "met."

She raised a brow at his word choice. "Is that what you call it?"

"Weel, we did meet at that point. Did we no'?"

He paused to look into her ocean-blue eyes and saw the twinkle in them. She jested with him.

He smiled. "I'll admit, 'twas no' the most ideal situation for a meeting. But I have no regrets. I'm glad I met ye."

She took a sip of ale, licking an errant drop of liquid on her lip. "I can honestly say that I'm happy our paths had crossed. I wish some of the circumstances were different. I could have done without the betrayal of my father. No, not my father," she corrected, and her feeling of sadness pulsed around them in the room.

"I'm verra sorry. Ye shouldna have had to find out that information that way."

She nodded. "Me too, but I'm glad I know. That makes my childhood make much more sense. Gives a reason as to why he treated me the way he did. I'm a bit surprised my mother kept the secret."

"We will sail ye home soon so ye can see yer mother and tell her of his…" He let the sentence trail off.

She tucked a lock of blonde hair behind her ear. "She most likely is aware already. Whoever my fa—James hired for the job surely contacted my mother to let her know what has happened."

"I'm sure ye still want to get home."

"You're going to accompany me there?"

"Aye, unless you wish me no' to?" His breath hitched.

"I would like you to come with me very much." She lifted her hand to feather her fingers against his cheek, and he leaned into her touch. Her skin ignited a fire in him.

He grasped her hand, and kissed the skin of her palm, as he raised his eyes to meet hers. She stared at him quietly. The blue of her eyes darkened to almost midnight. Was that wanting there in the depths?

He hoped so.

He brought his face closer to hers.

"Lass?" He whispered.

"Hmmm?" she asked, the question barely audible.

"I want to kiss ye."

Her eyes widened in surprise, and he heard her breath catch. "I would like that very much," she parroted her earlier sentence.

She didn't have to say it again. He captured her mouth in his, drawing her body nearer to his. His tongue brushed against her teeth, and he applied pressure, wordlessly asking for entry into the warm depths of her mouth.

She acquiesced, and his tongue slid inside. She tasted of ale and sweetness as she tentatively touched his tongue with hers. She sighed against his mouth, and his cock roared to life.

The kiss lasted longer than he intended, but he couldn't pull away from the warmth of her mouth. He wanted to taste her sweetness forever.

A sharp knock sounded on the door, and she quickly pushed away from him as if she'd been burned.

"Milady," called one of the maids from the other side of the door. "We've yer bathwater for ye."

Isobel looked at him in a panic, and he stood, walking over to the far wall and facing the window. The last thing he needed was for her or the maids to see him in the state he was in—hard for the woman who was chaotically trying to smooth her skirts.

"Milady? Is everything all right?"

Isobel cleared her throat, and he heard her take a deep breath before finally answering. "One moment, please." The rustle of her skirts sounded as she made her way to the door and allowed the maids in.

Lochlan turned to watch as the room filled with servants. Two lads, quite large in stature, carried in a tub and set it near the door. They moved the chairs out from in front of the fireplace and off to the side, and then picked up the tub once more and placed it in front of the hearth. She'd bathe by the firelight.

He caught his moan in his throat at the thought of her naked in the water, the shadows of the flames dancing on her skin.

Damn. He should leave. He knew that, but he couldn't make his feet budge. It was if they'd become part of the stone floor, rendering him immobile.

Bucket after bucket of steaming water was brought in and added to the tub. One maid came in with a stack of drying cloths and a cleansing bar scented with dried herbs.

The last pail of water was brought in, and the maid paused before Isobel. "Do ye need anything further, milady?" She asked, looking between Isobel and Lochlan.

He knew it was indecent for him to be in the room alone with Isobel, especially if she was going to take a bath, but he wasn't going anywhere. Not unless she told him to leave.

"Would ye like help with yer bath?" The maid asked, her gaze once again hopping from Lochlan to Isobel.

Isobel worried her lower lip with her teeth again as she gazed shyly at him. She was so beautiful.

Making up her mind, she walked the maid to the door. "I'll be fine. Thank you for the bath." She closed the door quietly behind her, and Lochlan's heart skipped a beat when he heard the lock click into place.

Isobel turned to look at him, her back against the door, palms flat against the wood. "I think we have much to discuss."

"Yer bath," he stated.

"It can wait."

"The water will be cooled. Ye'll catch a fever. I should leave." So much for his stand that he wouldn't leave unless she told him to.

"Please stay." Her voice was quiet, barely above a whisper.

He squeezed his eyes shut and heaved a sigh. "Lass, I dinna think ye know the effect ye are having on me. Ye should take yer bath whilst the water is still hot."

She nodded. "Will you help me?"

Her voice was even quieter than before when she asked this question. She bit her lip as she watched him.

It was a habit of hers he found he quite enjoyed.

"Ye dinna know what ye are asking, lass."

"I do." He watched as she approached him, tentatively. Her innocence was showing. He closed the distance between them and captured her mouth in his, wrapping his arms around her, crushing her to him.

She moaned, and he wanted nothing more than to tear off her gown and sink himself deep into her core. But he would not do that to her.

"Marry me, lass." The words were out of his mouth before he could think about what he was saying.

"Lochlan?" Her blue eyes implored his.

He sat on the floor and brought her with him, settling her on his lap, realizing that was not his best idea but trying to ignore his excitement.

"I ken I have no land or holdings to offer to ye, but I have coin. I can make a verra comfortable life for us. It doesna have to be on the sea—it can be wherever ye wish."

"You mean it?"

"Aye. With all my heart. From the first time I saw ye, I knew my life would never be the same."

He waited, watching emotions flicker over her beautiful features. Excitement. Worry. Concern.

"I can't accept your offer."

Lochlan felt as if he'd just taken a dirk to the gut. The searing burn of rejection was so strong. So painful. They weren't of the same mind.

She turned in his lap and faced him, the movement not helping the situation any. Her eyes bored into his as she reached up and tucked an errant strand of hair behind his ear before stroking his cheek and placing her lips against his.

He was so confused. He didn't press the kiss. He gave her control and waited.

"I can't accept your offer," she repeated, "until I learn why they call you Chaos." She smiled devilishly.

She was exasperating. He tickled her sides for making him think she didn't want him, and she giggled as she rolled away from him.

Breasts heaving, she laughed and pierced him with a bold, blue gaze. "I am serious. I want to know how you've come to be known as Chaos."

He laughed. "Aye, I'll tell ye the story. But first, take yer bath, lass."

"Will you be taking a bath as well?"

"I can go to my chambers and get one."

She shook her head. "Here."

One word.

But with such meaning.

Isobel stood in front of Lochlan as he trailed his fingers over her shoulder and between her breasts. Her breath caught in her throat. So many thoughts swirled in her mind.

She was going to be married.

To a pirate.

Named Chaos.

He tugged on the tie of her gown, and the material loosened. She tried to breathe, but her chest felt constricted. Lochlan pulled on the strands more, and her dress no longer held her shape.

He leaned down and captured her mouth in his once again. She never knew kissing could be such magic. But every time his lips touched hers, a warm tingle fluttered in her core. He pushed the dress off her shoulders, and the material pooled on the floor.

She stood before him in only her shift. She'd never felt so exposed. She lifted her arms to cover herself, and he clicked his tongue.

"Nay, lass. Never shield yerself from my eyes. Such beauty should never be hidden."

She flushed but did as she was told.

He stepped back and jerked his tunic over his head, tossing it away from them. Her eyes focused on the symbol on his chest. Without thought, she brought her hand up and traced the markings gently with her fingertips. She looked up and was met with blue eyes, dark as midnight watching her.

"I've never seen anything like this," she stated, her fingers still skimming the skin.

He captured her hand in his and kissed the tips of her fingers. "A memory from a long time ago. A tale for another time." He kissed the tip of her nose and unhooked his belt. She knew what was happening but was still unprepared when his breeches dropped to the floor.

Unable to stop herself, her eyes traveled down his broad chest, then lower to his navel, and even lower until they fell upon his manhood, standing turgid, and she swallowed hard.

There was nothing small about Lochlan MacLean.

He smiled as he bent his head and nuzzled her neck, grasping the thin material of her shift and gliding it over her head, depositing it in the same pile as his shirt and breeches. In one swift action, he swept her up in his strong arms and carried her over to the tub. Stepping into the water, he carefully sat down and settled her in front of him.

The water was no longer hot but still warm enough, and the heat radiating off of Lochlan's body scorched her skin wherever it touched his. He grabbed a hand-sized square of cloth, dipped it into the water, and then rubbed the cleansing bar until suds formed.

She sat stiffly, not knowing what to do with herself.

"Lass, relax," he cooed as he pushed her body forward a little and then stroked the cloth up and down her back, scrubbing her skin.

The gesture forced her buttocks back and she could feel his manhood touching her there.

She was both excited and terrified at the same time. Her parents—no, her mother might have, until recently, allowed her to choose her husband, but since she'd never had any suitable prospects, her mother and she had never discussed such things.

He began to massage her shoulders, and she couldn't resist leaning her head back and letting out a sigh. His strong fingers worked gently, easing the tension she had built up. His lips followed his fingers, placing soft kisses on each shoulder.

Then she remembered her demand.

She turned quickly and winced at both the look of pain that quickly crossed Lochlan's face at the sudden movement and the water that sloshed over the sides. She would clean that when they were finished. She didn't want to be a burden.

"What's wrong, lass?"

"You owe me an answer."

He raised a questioning brow and took one of her arms in his hands, drawing the soapy cloth back and forth. "To what?"

"Your name."

"Ah, right now? I can think of much more exciting things to occupy our time."

She snatched the cloth out of his hand and dipped it into the water, and brought it across his chest, watching as his muscles bobbed and constricted at her touch.

"I'm waiting," she drawled, skimming the cloth over his shoulders.

"Fine. 'Tis no' that interesting of a story and sounds much worse than it is."

"No matter. I still want to hear."

"My brothers and I were out on a mission."

"You have brothers?" She interrupted.

He put his finger to her lips. "Shh," he hushed her. "I dinna have brothers by blood. But they are my brothers just the same."

She was going to ask another question when he shook his head at her.

"Another story for another time, lass." He smiled and kissed her nose again.

She liked that motion. It seemed so playful from someone who looked so imposing and intimidating.

"On this mission, we had to go onto a farm. I'll spare ye the details, as most are uninteresting and uneventful. But in the end, I somehow managed to set all the animals free. Chaos ensued. Horses, hogs, cattle, chickens. Every animal on the farm was running loose. The noise awakened the owner, and our identities were almost made known. So we had to retreat. I've been known as Chaos ever since."

She remained quiet for a few long moments, then burst into laughter.

A look of confusion crossed his face. "What?"

"You got the scariest name from something so comical. A mistake. That's very funny."

He feigned hurt. "Many a man has cowered at the mention of my name."

"I'm sure they have. But they don't know the origin."

"All right. Enough of this," he teased. "The water's getting cool. Let's finish up." He helped her wash her hair, and she did the same to him. But then he brought the cloth to her breasts and swirled it around in sudsy circles.

She gasped at the sensation, and he chuckled, deep and low in his throat.

"Do ye like that?"

She wasn't sure she could form words, so she silently nodded her head.

He trailed the cloth down her belly and brought it between her legs, rubbing gently. Her breath quickened.

She never knew a bath could be so—her mind searched for the word—carnal. He finished washing her, and then after rinsing her off, he lifted her out of the tub and put a large linen cloth around her shoulders.

"Dry yerself and wait for me on the bed. I'll be right there."

Isobel did as she was told, watching Lochlan out of the corner of her eye as he hurriedly bathed and rinsed before stepping out of the tub, snatching a cloth and rubbing his chest and shoulders dry.

His massive size made the room seem small, which it wasn't. The fire cast an orange glow on his golden skin, and he was the most handsome man she'd ever laid eyes upon.

He approached slowly, his eyes dark pools as he drank her in.

"Dinna be scared, lass. I'll never hurt ye." He stopped in front of her, and she averted her eyes from his manhood that stood so prominently at attention.

He crouched and brought his lips to hers at the same time he picked her up and placed her in the center of the bed. He trailed kisses down the side of her neck, nipping at the tender skin there. She hissed.

He dropped his hand to her breast, the globe filling his palm before squeezing it slightly.

She cried out...breaking the kiss. She felt empty, but his mouth was soon on her breast, circling her nipple before sucking it into his mouth and gently grazing it with his teeth.

He kept up the torment as his other hand trailed down her side and over her stomach, through her nest of curls, and found her opening. She stiffened, and he whispered in her ear nonsensical words. Maybe something in his Scots language, she didn't know, but the words sounded beautiful as he spoke them, and she relaxed just a bit.

He laved first one breast and then the other, all the while her pulse quickened, and her heart beat out of her chest. His finger parted her slick folds and rubbed, up and down, up and down.

He kept repeating that motion, and then his thumb moved higher, and her buttocks lifted off the bed.

The sensation felt as if her skin were afire.

She opened her mouth on a moan, and he quickly covered it with his, his wicked tongue doing a delightful dance against hers.

She felt him push a finger inside her opening, and she gasped, but he swallowed it into his mouth and pushed his finger farther in before withdrawing it slowly. He carried on this torture with first one finger, then two, and then another.

She writhed on the bed, feeling almost feverish. Her body was so heated. She finally broke the kiss and just cried out, "Lochlan!"

He positioned himself on top of her, spreading her legs with his thighs. He looked down at her, and she could see the passion in his eyes.

"Are ye sure, lass?"

She nodded. She needed this. Needed him.

"'Twill hurt at the beginning."

She nodded again and tried to bring him down to her.

He was too strong and stayed resting on his elbows as he pressed his manhood against her core.

Her breath hitched, and she stiffened again. She didn't mean to.

But he felt it. "'Tis okay, lass," he cooed. He waited and watched her, and when she gave him a small smile, he captured her mouth in his again at the same time he pushed his length into her, breaching her barrier.

She cried out at the sudden, sharp pain. He paused his hips, holding himself up with his elbows still, and placed small kisses on her neck, his hands cradling her head.

"It should not last long, lass. 'Twill pass." All the while, he kept kissing her, showing her nothing but kindness, caring, and love. "My beautiful wife," he whispered.

Her heart nearly burst out of her chest as he said that line. Her body began to ache for him once again, longing for him to finish what he had started.

She clutched his buttocks and pulled him to her. She wasn't sure if that was what she was supposed to do, but he seemed to understand and slowly thrust into her once again, then drew slowly away and plunged forward again in a tantalizing rhythm that had her whole body humming.

"Isobel," he moaned, and she'd never heard anything so enticing.

His thrusts quickened, and she moved her hips in time with his.

He bowed his head to her breast once again and grazed her nipple with his teeth. When he did, she felt sparks fire all through her body as it contracted around him.

She whimpered his name, and his hold on her tightened as he squeezed his eyes shut, and with a final, deep thrust, he shivered his release into her. Both of them were breathing heavily and gulping for air.

He rolled onto his back, taking her with him, so she lay on his stomach, and she felt him slip out of her.

Opening her eyes, she saw him watching her with concern. She gave him a genuine smile and kissed his lips. "My husband," she murmured against his mouth.

CHAPTER 17

*T*he next day Isobel and Lochlan stood at the altar in the chapel located on the hill near Straik Castle.

Maggie was on Isobel's right side, and Broderick stood on Lochlan's left, as the priest in front of them recited the marriage vows.

How she wished her mother could be here to see the ceremony. But they would be traveling to England after their wedding. As Lochlan had told her, he didn't want to spend another day without her as his wife. So they'd talked with Maggie and Broderick as they broke their fast this morning, and their union had been quickly planned.

Beside her, Lochlan squeezed her hand, reassuringly. She looked up at him, and he blessed her with a charming, sincere smile.

Isobel knew her mother would like Lochlan and approve of the match once she understood the situation. She would have to explain all the events that had unfolded since he had attacked their traveling party what seemed like months ago but was only a matter of weeks.

How much her life had changed since then.

"I now pronounce ye man and wife."

Lochlan beamed as he enveloped her in a hug, his strong arms wrapping around her and drawing her in close.

"I love ye," he whispered near her ear.

"I love you," she countered.

"All right, ye two love birds," Broderick teased. "Enough of that. Just because ye are married now doesna mean we want to see ye both fawn over each other." His eyes twinkled as he spoke.

"Ignore him," Maggie said as she hugged Isobel. "I remember a time when he couldna keep his hands to himself as well."

"What do ye mean, ye remember a time?" Broderick asked, coming up behind his wife and patting her bottom as he kissed her cheek. He turned to Lochlan and clapped him on the shoulder. "Congratulations, Brother. Ye deserve a good woman like Isobel, even if she is English." He bellowed with laughter at her look of surprise.

"You were much nicer when I first met you," she derided.

Lochlan grabbed her around the waist and pulled her closer, nuzzling her neck. "And to think for a time, ye were conflicted as to who was the bigger gentleman."

The group laughed as they made their way out of the chapel. Isobel was quite sure the priest was uncomfortable with their open affection, and she was happy to leave and escape the walls of the small church.

Broderick and Lochlan began a conversation about the trip to England, and Maggie and Isobel let them walk ahead of them to discuss the navigation route they'd sail. The salt of the ocean hung heavy in the air as they walked, and it looked like a storm might be forming.

"Ye'll most likely wait for the storm to pass through before leaving," Maggie commented as if reading her mind.

"I hope so. My stomach isn't always the best on the water.

I get used to the constant rocking after some time, but it's hard at the beginning."

"I'm sure Lochlan will take that into consideration, especially now that ye're married. I'm verra happy for ye. And Lochlan. He deserves to be happy."

"I hope I can be what he needs."

Maggie smiled. "Ye already are."

~

That night, Lochlan sat in front of the hearth in his and Isobel's bedchamber and watched as she readied herself for bed.

He'd never seen anyone as beautiful as her, and he thanked the lord above for the treasure he'd been given.

The whisky in his belly—a wedding present from Broderick and Maggie—relaxed him, and the warmth of the fire added to his already heated skin.

She finished brushing her long, blonde hair and came and sat on his lap, wrapping her arms around his neck and kissed his cheek.

"Ye ready for bed?" he asked.

"To sleep?"

"Sleep will come later, lass." He smiled devilishly as he lifted her in his arms and carried her to the bed.

"But I'm tired now," she jested.

"I know just the thing to wake ye up," he answered, slipping her shift up her body and exposing her breasts. He kissed her deeply and cupped her breasts, massaging the pillowy globes. Their size fit perfectly in his hands. He flicked his thumb over her nipples, and her body jerked under him.

He smiled against her mouth and broke the kiss, nibbling his way down her chin, then her neck, and the valley between her breasts. He suckled each bud into his mouth before continuing his trail of kisses.

Lower.

Lower.

He positioned himself so that her legs rested on his shoulders and he blew a hot breath onto the nest of damp curls.

"Lochlan."

"Hmmm?" he said against her nether region, knowing she would enjoy the sensation.

"Lochlan!" she gasped.

He laughed and used his hands to spread her folds and licked her delicious sweetness. Her fists clenched in his hair as she squeezed her legs in response. His spitfire wife was a treasure indeed. He pushed a finger into her warm depths and slowly slid it back and forth as he continued to lap at her.

Her pants grew louder, and his cock grew harder.

Her legs clamped down harder the closer she got to her release, and just before he thought she would climax, he tore his mouth away from her and sank his length into her on a moan that he felt in his soul.

Within moments, her inner core was clenching around his length, and he couldn't last any longer. He grasped her hips and thrust hard and fast, his release coming on a gasp of her name.

He stayed there for a long moment, savoring the feel of her in his arms, before slipping out of her and laying on his back, drawing her body close to his. He grabbed a throw and pulled it over them.

"Now ye can sleep, lass," he said and kissed her forehead.

EPILOGUE

*I*t took the *Hella* almost two days to sail to England. The storm that they had thought they'd waited out long enough came back with a vengeance on their journey. Isobel had surprised herself and managed to keep the contents of her stomach in her stomach and not over the rails.

She'd say that was progress.

"Please let me talk to Mother first before you say anything, Lochlan," she said, placing a hand on his chest.

He clasped her hand and kissed her fingers. "I dinna need ye to fight for me, Isobel. I'm quite capable of handling myself."

She sighed. "I know. But you forget my mother hasn't seen me in some time, and the last time she did, it was with you dragging me away from her, and your men locking her in her carriage. She doesn't even know if I'm alive."

"She does."

She looked at her husband, his mouth set in a grim line. "How?"

"I sent word. I didna want her fashing herself sick with worry over ye. She needed to know ye were safe."

Isobel's heart swelled at how thoughtful and caring her husband was. She was learning things about him that surprised her every day.

"You did?"

"Aye," he answered as if it that gesture was something anyone would do.

The front door swung open before Isobel and Lochlan even reached the entry.

"Isobel!" her mother cried as she ran forward and enveloped her in a warm hug. Her mother clung to her as if her life depended on it. "I'm so sorry. I didn't know." She held her by the shoulders at arm's length, so she could look her over to make sure Isobel was indeed well.

"I know, Mother. I'm fine, really."

Lochlan held back as they had their reunion, keeping his distance. She was surprised. She didn't expect him to listen to her.

"Mother." She took a step back. "I'd like you to meet my husband, Lochlan MacLean." She wrung her hands together, not knowing how her mother was going to react. "I know the first and last time you met him was not on the best of terms, but—"

Her mother cut her off and approached Lochlan, then dipped low into a curtsy, "Sir MacLean. How can I ever repay you?"

Well, that wasn't the reception she'd expected Lochlan to receive. It was a very surprising day, indeed.

"I am no sir, Lady Anne, and I've already received the greatest gift. My wife." He smiled, and Isobel thought her mother was going to melt into the man.

"I know the first time we met, the circumstances were not

ideal. But I've learned much since that day. About my daughter and how strong she is. About my husband, and the lengths he would go to for his greed. And about the man my daughter has married. Without me, I might add."

"I do apologize for that, milady. The marriage wasna forced upon her."

She dismissed his latter statement with a wave of her hand. "I know that. As I've stated, I've learned a lot in the time my daughter has been away. It seems my own loyalties have been misplaced. You've protected my daughter. From her ill-gotten betrothed. From her fath—from James. From so many things that I didn't even know were a worry. And you've made her very happy. I can see it in the way she looks at you. And if she's happy, I'm happy. For that, I am in your debt, and unlike my former husband, I repay my debts. I just have one question."

"Anything, milady."

"Scotland or England?"

"Pardon?"

"I think it's quite simple. Which would you rather if you had a choice? Scotland or England?"

Lochlan's gaze locked with Isobel's and she could see the internal war he fought with himself. Choose his beloved Scotland and mayhap make her miserable, or choose England, and he himself be miserable. After the time Isobel had spent in Scotland, she didn't mind the landscape. If that was what he wanted to choose, she wouldn't complain.

"Choose what is in your heart, Lochlan. What will make you the happiest."

"Wherever you are is where I will be most happy."

"And I, you. Let your heart lead your decision, and I will follow."

Relief seemed to relax his shoulders. "Scotland, milady."

"Scotland it is, then, Laird MacLean."

"Excuse me?" Lochlan asked in disbelief.

"As payment for protecting my daughter and making her happy, you will receive what was originally offered tenfold. You are now Laird MacLean of Redstone Castle in Lunan Bay, Scotland. I had a feeling that you would choose Scotland, so I already had the papers drawn. They just await your signature."

Isobel jumped into his arms. "You've done it!" She plastered kisses on his face.

"I dinna believe it. Are ye sure?"

"I will do anything to protect my daughter, and from what it appears, so will you. For that, no coin would ever be enough. So, I will grant you your legacy."

"I, I," he stammered, setting Isobel back on her feet and bowed deeply to Lady Anne. "I thank ye, milady."

"And I, you. Now, sign the papers, and we shall finalize this. And then you can go and give me the grandchildren I want to see."

Isobel laughed as Lochlan swept her up into another hug.

She shivered when he whispered in her ear, "But ye're still my most precious treasure. I love ye, Lady Isobel MacLean."

As she listened to his declaration, she knew it to be true. She wasn't sure when the exact moment was when her captor became her savior, but here they were.

And she knew they had a bright future ahead of them.

Never in her wildest dreams would she have thought being captured by a mercenary would be the best thing that ever happened to her.

His stormy blue eyes met hers, and he dipped his head, taking her mouth in a fierce kiss that screamed *mine*.

And she was. Now and forever.

. . .

If you enjoyed *A Pirate's Treasure*, please consider leaving a review at the retailer where you purchased this book to help the Scottish Rogues of the High Seas series grow.

A PIRATE'S WRATH

SCOTTISH ROGUES OF THE HIGH SEAS, BOOK 2

A strong-willed woman. A ruthless pirate. Their formidable bond.

Seonag Ruane never believed her father died in an ambush. She knows he was betrayed by men he trusted. Driven by her mother's grief and her own need for vengeance, Seonag will do whatever it takes to discover the truth. Even risk her own life. Her plan for revenge never included falling in love with the sweet-tongued pirate who shared his secrets late at night.

Captain Colin Harris's closest friend was killed by his mutinous crew. He vows to avenge his fellow pirate's death by seeking retribution and recovering the bounty the ship was transporting. It's the least he can do for the family left behind. His mission is compromised when he discovers the lad he recently hired is actually a woman in disguise and their mutual bond of trust is broken. Angered by her deceit, he imprisons the masquerader.

Seonag is certain she's failed in her quest to destroy those responsible for her father's death. How will she forgive the one man she thought she could trust? Unable to dismiss the powerful pull of attraction toward the lass, Colin decides to free her, only to learn too late that she has been captured. Worse he discovers that she is his late friend's daughter. Will he get to her before his mistake takes away the one woman that might make him whole?

Order A PIRATE'S WRATH now: https://amzn.to/3yGSRta

ALSO BY BRENNA ASH

Contemporary Romance

Second Chances

Paranormal Romance

A Kiss of Stone

ABOUT THE AUTHOR

Brenna Ash is addicted to coffee and chocolate. When she's not writing, she can be found either poolside reading a book, or in front of the TV, binge-watching her favorite shows, *Outlander* and *Sons of Anarchy*. She lives in Florida with her husband and a very, very spoiled cat named Lilly. She loves to interact with her readers on social media. Please feel free to follow her at the following platforms:

www.facebook.com/BrennaAshAuthor
www.twitter.com/brenna_ash
www.pinterest.com/brenna1168
www.instagram.com/BrennaAshAuthor

To stay up to date on all things Brenna Ash, including book news, release dates and contest info, please sign-up for her newsletter on her website.

www.BrennaAsh.com

Made in USA - North Chelmsford, MA
1306595_9781955677011
02.25.2022 1105